Butta Brown

By

Coco Mixon

Butta Brown

© 2014 Coco Mixon

Published by Coco Mixon

First Edition

Contributing Author: Coco Mixon

Cover Design: Drea Delgado

Editor: Coco Mixon & Shonda Wade

Acknowledgments:

I again humbly thank the most highest, without you there would be no existence. Thank you to my soulmate for everything you do and taught me. I thank my children for allowing me free time to write. To my parents; I would like to thank my parents for instilling great values in me. You guys continue to amaze me. Next, to my siblings; I appreciate each and every one of you.

Also I would like to thank Creative Flow Publications for all the love and support; yes my team ROCKS! Last and certainly not least, I want to thank my supporters; you are my career. Without your support there would be no career, and for that I am forever grateful.

A Special shout out to Shaniqua and Yolanda, you ladies are AWESOME.

Coco Mixon

Email: *authormisscoco@aol.com*

creativeflowpublishing@yahoo.com

Twitter: *@sweetcocokisses*

Facebook: *www.facebook.com/coco.mixon*

www.facebook.com/authormisscoco

www.facebook.com/creativeflowpublications

Butta Brown

By

Coco Mixon

BUTTA

I had been born for at least a week and my father hadn't stopped by, or at least that's the story I always heard. It was always told that he missed the first week of my life; I never held it against him because he always made an effort to be part of my life.

My dad took me on fishing trips, amusement park adventures, and more. He even paid for me to attend a special youth CSI course. I knew he was the coolest dad ever. There was nothing anyone could tell me about Charles Brown that could change my mind about how great he was, but one day that changed; I'll get to that shortly.

****

My mom was a cute caramel complexion, with an hour glass figure. Men always tried to get her attention but she only had eyes for my daddy. Karen was her name and I miss her daily. She stayed true to my dad until the day she passed away.

My dad didn't live with us, but he made sure I was taken care of and we wanted for nothing. I'm not sure how he made all his extra money, but it was like money grew on trees when he was around. He would splurge and get me everything I wanted.

I remember when I was like twelve and all I wanted was to play basketball for the park. My mom told me it cost too much, but low and behold I called my dad and the next day I was receiving my jersey. My dad was like that, he made things happen.

Once I started in the league Coach Johnson always had me running extra drills and laps. It was like he hated me. Some kids say my dad was sleeping with Coach Johnson's wife, but I was a kid I had nothing to do with that.

"I'm tired, I don't want to run another lap coach," I whined.

"Are you a man or a mouse?" Coach asked me.

"A man?" I replied more with a questioned toned then contentment.

"Then finish your laps like a man," he ordered.

"No one else have to do it," I continued to whine.

It was obvious the coach was annoyed by my comments because he added on a hundred and fifty push-ups. I was damn near in tears. I couldn't wait to get home and tell my mama how unfair I was being treated.

"Mama….Mama," I called out as I ran in the house full of tears.

"Coach hates me. He makes me run drills while everyone else relaxes," I cried.

"We'll just see about that," I heard my dad say from behind me.

I hadn't even noticed my dad was there, but I was glad he was. Hearing him speak assured me that the coach would treat me better than he has been treating me. He gave me a huge hug and my mom wiped my tears away. Part of me wanted the coach to get hit by a bus, but something inside me said it was wrong but my mind told me it was right.

The next day when I arrived at practice they told us practice was cancelled until further notice. The coach had been killed in his sleep. He was murdered by affixation. I wasn't sure what that meant but I made a mental note to look it up. I ran home in a happier mood than I arrived at the park in, today was a glorious day.

"The coach is dead," I yelled once I entered the house.

My mom looked at my dad and shook her head. I didn't know why but I laughed anyway. I was silly like that. Everything made me laugh, no matter if I was happy or sad; I was laughing. It usually kept me in trouble instead of out of trouble.

****

I grew up in Compton, a small city in California. Back in the 80's it was filled with thugs and drugs. I didn't mind, because I didn't know any better. The hood was all I knew my dad kept me in all kinds of activities hoping to keep me from the gang life. He always assured me that one day I wouldn't need a clique, because I already had one. I never knew what that meant until I got older; well a few years later I actually found out more about my dad.

BUTTA

I hadn't seen my dad in over a week; yeah I talked to him but he hadn't physically come by in over a week. My mom assured me that he was fine, and he was dealing with some issues. I was almost sixteen, so my big concern was would he be around for my birthday. Again they assured me he would be.

When my birthday rolled around, I had a nice gathering at the park, but my dad only attended for a few hours. That made me angry in a sense but I tried not to let it ruin my birthday. I was determined for this to be the best year of my life.

Since my dad left early I decided to disappear as well. I made my way to the liquor store in the hood. I was in need of some White Owl cigars. The local store in the neighborhood sold to teens all the time; therefore I knew I wouldn't get carded. I already had my weed so the cigars were my only missing necessity.

When I was exiting the store I saw this female staring at me. I was going to ignore her because all I wanted to do was get high, but she asked me my name and at that very moment my life changed. When she said she was a Brown, I had to pause because she kind of looked like me and my daddy.

We exchanged numbers and I wanted to investigate. While she was contacting her grandmother I asked my mom. My mom only response was, "Call your dad." That alone confirmed my suspicions that Pepper was indeed my sister.

She didn't contact me for a few days. I believe our dad confessed to both of us on the same day; unfortunately he was still harboring secrets. Since I grew up an only child I was excited to have a sibling. Pepper and I hooked up immediately and realized we were just alike. No one could touch the Brown siblings, we were inseparable. I loved having a little sister to protect and she loved having a big brother to protect her. We had begun doing everything together.

I was a little mad at my dad for not telling me, but I was so excited to have a sibling I honestly overlooked it. When I found out my little sister Pepper lived not too far from me, it was even better.

About a week later I decided to go to the Slauson Swap Meet. Typically I would have gone to the one in Compton, but this particular day I just wanted to get away. I didn't have a car, so I rode the RTD to L.A.

When I arrived, bitches were everywhere, and L.A. hoes were a little bit different than the bitches in Compton and Long Beach. I was intrigued. I strolled around and copped me a few T-shirts, and a few packs of socks. As I headed to the concession area to get some chili cheese fries, I noticed there was a commotion.

Immediately I checked my pocket for my knife, and flicked my tongue to make sure my blade was secure. I wasn't a L.A. nigga so I needed to be prepared in case these muthafucka's tried something.

The closer I got to the concession area; it was obvious it was a bunch of bitches arguing. Instead of being nosey, I ordered my food and proceeded to head out. But there was something drawing me to the commotion.

After busting a U-turn I walked towards the drama. At that point I noticed it was two girls arguing and a one bitch nigga in the middle. I was about to shrug it off, until I noticed one of the girls was my baby sister.

I bust through the crowd ready for war, and as I went to grab my sister out of the circle, she went crazy on me. I decided not to battle her and walk away. In my mind we had just met and she wasn't feeling having a brother.

Feeling defeated I exited the shopping center and made my way home. I exited the bus in the city; Compton that is, and decided to go to the liquor store.

"Hey big bro," I heard as I entered the store.

I was a little baffled because she just snubbed me at the Swap Meet. Then I noticed she had on a completely different outfit.

"Yeah, hey... Wait a minute, how did you change and beat me back to the City?" I wondered.

"Huh?" she replied.

"And what the fuck was up with you at the Swap Meet?" I asked.

"Negro, are you crazy?" she laughed.

We sat there going back and forth until she explained to me she absolutely did not go to the Swap Meet. The next thing she said changed my life. She told me our dad had cancer and we had other siblings.

"You think that was our sister I saw today?" I asked.

"All I know is we are supposed to look alike, or at least that's what daddy said," Pepper replied.

I was a little pissed my dad didn't disclose this information to me. Did he have a closer bond with Pepper or his other kids? I was really lost in my thoughts, until my sister drug me out of the store.

We went back to my house to smoke. My house was a cool chill spot since my mom worked long hours. Pepper and I grabbed some Chinese food and went to the house and smoked ourselves into a frenzy.

We called our grandmother and she confirmed what Pepper said. I was even more shocked to find out Carlos was the oldest. I wanted to reach out to them but my dad had instructed us not to. We were calling him at Grandma's house consistently. I hated he was barely home.

Pepper and I decided to put my training to use. We found our siblings and I basically followed them to try and learn more about them. I was intrigued with both of them. They had actually just found out about each other as well.

It was amazing to see how much we all looked alike, especially the girls. My dad had some strong genes. Part of me wanted to reach out to them, but instead I'll play the position my dad gave me.

PEPPER

When I first saw Butta my heart immediately told me he was related to me. I never imagined he would be my brother. It amazed me even more knowing there was others. When my dad confessed he had cancer, he told me a lot of his secrets. He said I was the only one he knew wouldn't judge him.

He said my sister and other brother was a lot more pissed than Butta and I. Personally I was hurt my dad had a whole secret life, but I loved him so much he could have told me the sun was purple and I would have believed it.

Daddy had Butta trained with so many skills and I was prepared to use them all. I had every connect I could think of watching them. The only thing I didn't care for was how my dad wanted his other daughter Chocolate to not know about me. It was like he was protecting her feelings but mines were expendable.

"Brother you think daddy love them more?" I wondered as we sat on the park bench.

"I'm not sure, but what I do know is this is some good ass weed," he laughed.

That was my big brother; he was always smiling or laughing. You could tell him you just got shot and a smile would creep on his face. He was just that silly and easy going.

Now my mean ass was another story. I just didn't give a fuck. I popped off at the drop of a dime. My temper sometimes was uncontrollable and I often fought the urge to gut a nigga.

A few hours later Butta and I parted ways. We were headed back to our boring and normal sibling-less lives. I was walking towards my house when I heard my name called.

"Oh Lord, what do you want Kevin?" I shook my head.

"What's up sexy?" he smiled.

"Fool what do you want?" I smiled.

"Wanna smoke?" he asked while holding up a baggie of that sticky icky.

My pot-head ass couldn't resist, so instead of going home, I took my ass back to Kevin's house. Now Kevin was a local hood nigga that everybody thought was sexy. Every bitch wanted to be with him and every nigga wanted to be him. He was as smooth as my daddy. So I just couldn't resist him.

When we got back to his spot, he rolled up a couple and poured us a drink. I wasn't a huge drinker but I could hold my own. We were really getting our buzz on and Kevin was flirting his ass off.

I was feeling it but I didn't like all the touchy feely shit. Now I love me some dick, but don't think just because you have one I want it.

"So are you gonna let me fuck?" he blurted.

"Hahahahaha, nigga really?" I laughed.

"You smoking my weed and drinking my liquor," he casually replied.

"True, but it is for us to chill. Chilling does not equal you getting my pussy," I stated.

I continued puffing on the blunt and sipping my drink, because this nigga couldn't be serious. Before I knew that fool had jumped on top of me; and he was trying to force his tongue in my mouth. He also consistently began to fondle my breast.

I struggled to get him off of me, as he continued to overpower me. Kevin was trying to get my shorts off, as I fought him off of me. The next thing that happened shocked me. I have no clue where he came from, but Butta snatched Kevin off of me, punched him a few times before slicing his face severely with a razor.

"You okay sis?" he smiled.

"Yes I am big bro," I smirked.

When I saw the blood oozing from Kevin it gave me life. I sprang into action and I picked up a bat he had by the door. I repeatedly beat him upside his head. Brain matter splattered everywhere, but it felt so good I continued to hit him.

I didn't know what my next move would be, but I was grateful for my brother. He held me in a bear hug until I calmed down. He sat me in a corner for more than an hour as he did the most professional cleaning job I had ever seen.

Butta didn't discard the body; he just tampered with the scene enough that any detectives would have a hard time finding a killer. My brother was that damn good.

He cleaned me up to the best of his ability and we hot-tailed it out of there. Once we got back to his house, he gave me a t-shirt and a pair of his sweats to change into. I never saw the clothes I was wearing that day again.

"I can't believe you were there to save me," I cried.

"You're my little sister Pep, I will always be there," he embraced me.

I laid my head down on his chest and for the first time I was vulnerable in my brother's arms. It was a wonderful feeling that I could get used to.

That day we vowed to always have each other's back and no one could break our sibling bond. Life was just how it should have always been.

****

Months had gone bye and things were going great with me and Butta. It was weird because apparently our mothers knew each other but never told us about each other. It really didn't bother me that my mom didn't tell me, due to the fact she was always doing her own thing.

When people discovered Butta was my brother, people started treating me different. Yea I had a reputation as a fighter but having Butta as a brother, brought something else to the table.

I swear bitches loved him and niggas feared him; even the ones who wanted to be him. He was tall with light caramel skin; well his complexion was a matter of opinion. In my eyes he was a light caramel, but some people just called him light. His skin was smooth and flawless.

Butta was tall with a somewhat muscular exterior. He reminded me of my daddy so much. Especially with his smooth dressing skills. Butta was always dressed to kill; literally.

BUTTA

It was great having a little sister, but constantly having to watch niggas was tiring. My little sister was a gorgeous chocolate thang, and I would be damned if one of these bum as niggas played her.

I stopped hanging with my boys so much, because I chose to hang with my sister. I hadn't had a sister my whole life so we definitely had to make up for lost time. Part of me wanted to cuss my dad out, but in all honesty I was scared.

Even though we found out we were siblings my dad still never spent time with the both of us at the same time. I tried popping up at Pep's house when she said he was coming and the nigga kept driving. Maybe he was scared we would double team him with questions.

One great thing is Grandma was happy to spend time with the both of us; it was like she was finally releasing a burden off her shoulders. The only issue I had was on certain days she requested we didn't come over. We respected her wishes, well to a certain extent. I was good at spy tactics thanks to my dad sending me to special youth police training camps.

She spent some time with a young mixed boy, whom I assumed to be Carlos and sometimes I would see a Pepper looking female there on the days we were told not to visit, which must have been Chocolate.

GRANDMA LOUISA

My son Charlie was really stressing me out, spending time with all these different women and having all these babies. I was tired of the charade, and pretending I only had two grandchildren. I obliged my son the best I could because I loved him, but all this lying needed to stop.

He had multiple children running around the same cities and didn't know each other. I tried explaining to him that this wasn't a good look, but this boy swore the ladies loved him and couldn't resist him.

To some degree I knew he was telling the truth, because the little heifers always popped up at my door pregnant and crying for his love.

What they didn't know was Charlie was married and had his own home. He lied to all his women, and children except one about where he lived.

Charlie actually lived with his wife and eldest daughter. They had a picture perfect life in their minds, but neither knew the man they worshipped lived a huge lie.

My son was like a nymphomaniac he just loved women. Ever since he was little he loved women. By the time he was in junior high school, the neighborhood girls started flocking to my door.

It was non-stop, and then the lying started in high school. He met and fell in love with my granddaughter Chocolate's mother, they eventually married. Even though he was head over heels in love with MaryAnn it didn't stop him from sleeping around, thus fathering multiple children.

MaryAnn had beaten plenty of female's asses over Charles Brown Jr. and she knows all our family business. That's what made her a keeper in his eyes; she was loyal.

With years passing, I was getting old and the kids were older and wiser. It was easy for them to discover their dad's infidelity, because in his older years he was slipping.

Every time a grandchild found out, I confessed; shit I was tired of lying. I know I raised him better than that.

"Hi Grandma," Butta and Pepper spoke in unison.

"Hey babies, what brings you by?" I wondered.

"Where is our daddy?" Pepper wondered.

I gave the same lie I always gave; he was at work. Truth be told he was at home or with one of his other kids they didn't know about. He spread his time thin. He worked hard and hustled harder.

"He needs a pager," Pepper stated.

"Yeah, it's hard contacting him," Butta added.

I let the children know I would try and contact him to the best of my ability. We continued to visit for another hour before we said our goodbyes.

BUTTA

It had been a week since I last seen my father and I wasn't mad. I just knew something was up. My grandmother wasn't telling us anything and Pep damn sure didn't know anything.

It was a Tuesday afternoon; I had finally chosen to hang with my boys from the neighborhood. We were in my house getting high as fuck and playing NBA Jams when my phone rang.

"Speak to me," I said.

"Hey babe, you busy?" she wondered.

"Chilling," was my simple reply.

"The paramedics just brought Mr. Brown in," she paused.

When she paused I dropped the blunt. I didn't know what to say. Here was this grown woman I was smashing telling me, my dad was just brought into the hospital. She said she didn't know the details but thought I should know.

After kicking everyone out of my house I rushed to the hospital. I didn't call anyone, not my mom, my grandma, or my sister. I was only trying to get to my father.

When I arrived the chick I was fucking allowed me in the back to visit my dad. She said he requested for the hospital not to notify any family members.

"Daddy," I stated like a child.

"Butta? What are you doing here?" he wondered.

"No, what are you doing here?" I replied.

My dad confessed to me he was extremely ill and stated if he died to look after my siblings. He even stated we all had a role. I was taken aback because I had never met my other siblings.

I didn't dig much deeper, but I kept a mental note in my head. I stayed as long as my dad allowed me, and then went home. I was holding a heavy dose of reality in my mind and my dad wanted it to be a secret. Though he didn't tell me what his ailments were, it was obvious it was terminal.

I spent most of my night listening to the Dogg Pound CD and smoking. My mom didn't say much about me smoking in the house, just as long as I left her the hell alone while she was reading.

The next morning my little sister came over all in tears and boy I wasn't ready for the shit she had to say. Life was all fucked up.

PEPPER

"Daddy is in the hospital," I cried.

"I know Pep, I know," he hugged me.

"Nigga you know," I barked.

"I found out last night," he replied?"

"Last night?" I yelled.

I didn't give him a chance to respond. I was so pissed that he knew our dad was ill and didn't tell me. I pulled back from his embrace and began swinging.

I hit Butta in his arm and he laughed, it was when I rocked his chin that he body slammed my ass on the couch. That didn't stop my little ass from trying to give it to him. I wanted somebody to feel my pain.

"Stop Pepper before I hurt you," he huffed.

"Nigga you better hope I don't hurt you," I stated.

My brother pinned me down until I calmed down. That little nigga was strong. I knew I had some strength but he had me incapacitated.

"You calm?" he asked.

"Nope," I smirked.

He began tickling me until tears fell from my eyes. I was laughing so hard I damn near urinated in my pants. My brother was silly as hell. I loved having him around.

****

The next day my father signed the papers to be released against doctors wishes. He had me meet him at his house. My grandmother was out of town visiting God knows who. But this particular day, my daddy dropped some bombs on me.

"Baby-girl I have Cancer," he reiterated.

"Huh? What?" I mumbled.

"I have stage 4 Cancer. My body is tired Pumpkin," he stated.

"I don't understand daddy," I cried.

He continued to tell me he had been ill for some time and his body was weary. I know it sounds selfish, but I wanted my daddy to fight and never leave me. But his next confession threw me for a loop.

"Pumpkin, I have something for all of your siblings," he confessed.

I didn't know what to do or what to say. I sat there just listening to all of his confessions. He told me about how much a hoe he really was, and he wasn't husband material.

I begged my dad for my sister and brothers information but he only handed me four letters. He said when and if he died to give one to each of my siblings. I didn't know why he chose me, but I would do anything for my daddy, and that's what I did; I held his secrets.

He told me when the time came we would all officially meet and we all had a role to play. His comments baffled me but I took it all in.

****

That day when I told Butta about daddy being sick and he said he knew, I assumed he knew about our letters from daddy so I didn't spill the beans to him. He was confused and a little upset that daddy didn't want us to contact them.

"So he is basically dying and we still can't contact them until he dies?" Butta asked.

"That's what he said," I replied.

Butta was not happy at all, instead he used all the training my dad gave him to research our siblings and he wasn't going to stop until he got the information he wanted.

My brother was adamant on finding out everything about them. There was so much we didn't know about them and he was intrigued.

BUTTA

The more we talked about our untouchable siblings had me all into my feelings. I loved my dad but couldn't believe he kept them from us. I just wanted to know my siblings. My sister begged me to oblige my dad's wishes, and I did. All I wanted to do was see them.

I decided to just get the basic information on them. Once my grandmother showed me pictures, I did the basic tracking. I followed their every move.

My sister Chocolate looked just like Pepper or I guess Pepper looks like Chocolate since she is technically older. I was so excited to see her the first time, and then it dawned on me she was the girl I thought was Pepper that day at the swap meet.

My sister was just as feisty as Pepper. Just the time I had her under surveillance, I saw her go from zero to one hundred in a matter of moments. She was a bit more level headed than Pepper though.

Now my big brother on the other hand was my daddy all day. That nigga was severely hot headed. Everything pissed him off. His name is Carlos and he is part Hispanic. He is the lightest one of all of us, yet we all looked damn near identical.

I always tried to stay undetected, so I wore dark colors and hoodies while staying in the shadows. I learned a lot about them. I wasn't sure if they grew up together or not, but they seem just as close as Pep and I; if not closer.

They seemed to be a force to be reckoned with too. I really like how they got down. I wanted all of us to be bonded so strong.

When I asked my dad he said it wasn't the right time and they were no longer speaking to him. Apparently they didn't take his lies as lightly as Pepper and I did.

He told me they completely washed their hands on him and since he was ill Chocolate was coming around, but Carlos was still pretty angry.

I didn't know Carlos and couldn't understand why he was so angry. Charles was my dad too and I wasn't

pissed they existed. I was actually
happy. I liked having siblings.

CHARLES

My kids all were pretty special to me and I would do anything to make them happy. I managed to keep my past a secret as long as I could but you know the saying, what's done in the dark eventually comes to light.

I chose to confess to Pepper because I definitely didn't want her to hate me like Choc does. That shit hurt to my core knowing my kids are disgusted with me.

I treat all my kids equal to a certain degree. The only one that had me full time was Chocolate. She had the privilege of having me all the time, because I married her mother. I loved MaryAnn since the day I met her, and vowed to give her a life she deserved.

Unfortunately for her I was and still am a male gigolo. I love women! I promised her my infidelities wouldn't cause our home drama, and well that was a lie.

She kicked me out months ago when she learned about my son Carlos, how could I tell her I fathered two more, and possibly others. There was no possible way, and I vowed to take it to the grave; and Cancer is allowing death to come faster. I wonder if I'm being punished for my ways.

****

As the days grew, more weeks passed and my health was getting worse. All I wanted was my mommy. Instead the sicker I got the closer it brought my wife and my baby mama;

Carlos' mom, the only one she knew about.

We were all living as one happy family, even though Carlos wasn't speaking to me. Whenever I had a surge of energy I had a friend take me to see Butta and Pepper. Unfortunately those visits were few and far between.

It didn't take long before I needed to be hospitalized and I knew my kids would eventually all be together and MaryAnn would know the man she loved lived a complete lie the entire twenty years I've known her.

I had a substantial amount of money put away and had multiple life insurance policies. I made Carlos beneficiary on all policies since he was the oldest, and I knew he would do what was best for all his siblings. I even paid cash for them a nice big house, with enough rooms for each kid.

No matter how mad he was at me I knew Carlos heart wouldn't allow him to hate his siblings. He would do right by them and pick up where I left off. Butta was just as old as Los but joked about everything, therefore I only left everything to Carlos.

My days are numbered on this earth but I'm grateful for my wife and my side piece. They have taken real good care of a nigga. Their only concern was that our kids didn't inherit my hoe ways or my murderous ways.

Yeah a nigga had a bad temper. I made a living out of it too. A few people heard about my skills and had no problem with paying for my services to get rid of a nigga. I've done it since I was a kid. My dad taught me what he knew but honestly it's in my blood, because a few of our distant relatives had the same issue.

No matter what MaryAnn and Maria wanted I knew my children possessed the same qualities. I just did my best to keep them out of the family business.

When Butta questioned me about my lifestyle, I didn't tell him everything, I only told him what I wanted him to know. I knew he was investigating me, and he should put that expensive training to use. I returned back to the home I now shared with my wife and my side piece, where the air became too thin and I found myself hospitalized.

PEPPER

One of my brother's friends worked at the hospital. She was really cool; we even told people we were related. When she called me, I thought we would have a casual conversation, but instead she shocked my life.

"Hey hoe," I sang into the phone.

"Pep, y'all need to get to the hospital," she replied.

"What's up boo?" I wondered.

"They just rushed Mr. Brown in," she answered.

"My daddy?" I asked.

I knew she meant my daddy, but I had to ask to be sure. My emotions were all over the place I honestly didn't know what to do. My heart raced as I heard her calling my name. I didn't reply I just hung up, and immediately called Butta, and his response had me feeling like he already knew.

"Daddy is in the hospital," I cried.

"What?" he questioned.

Once what I said sunk in, he headed my way to pick me up. When we got to the hospital we debated what to do, because we saw my sister and some ladies with her. I assumed it was she and Carlos' mothers.

I wanted to oblige my dad's wishes but we deserved to be in there just as much as Chocolate did. I didn't see Carlos at first, and then noticed him come a little later.

We knew Carlos wasn't speaking to our dad, so when he came it had to be serious. I waited five more minutes before I said fuck it and went in. There was no way in Hell I was going to keep wondering if my dad was okay.

When I entered the emergency room, I heard loud sobbing. The closer I got I saw Chocolate wailing on the floor. My heart sank because I knew something was wrong.

Hearing the doctors speak made my horrible nightmare a reality. I was at such a loss of words. Part of me wanted to run away but I had to speak.

"Please don't tell me my daddy is dead," I stated.

It was like the room was in slow motion. All their tears came to a screeching halt. I could tell they were shocked. Reality was I was Charles' daughter. I looked just like Chocolate.

Carlos shook his head before he spoke, "Mr. Double Life strikes again."

I literally saw anger in his eyes. He would have probably got daddy up so he could kill him. Chocolate rose off the floor and came towards me. I prepared to fight, because shit they didn't seem accepting, but she extended her hand.

"Hi, I'm Chocolate, your sister, and this is Carlos our brother."

I laughed because she looked just like me. It was amazing how much we looked alike. I just couldn't believe it.

"I'm sorry you look just like me. I'm Pepper, Pepper Brown."

"I guess I was the only one with a regular name," Carlos angrily laughed.

I watched the two older ladies huddle up and confer. I knew they were wondering where I came from and who my mother was, but I didn't owe them an explanation.

We took some time to get to know each other, before their mothers offered to buy us breakfast. When we got to Denny's it was obvious they wanted to pick my brain, and I wasn't having it. Plus Butta was still outside watching us. He had followed us from the hospital to the restaurant.

I noticed Chocolate's mom watching Butta outside. I pretended to check my pager then excused myself and told my siblings I would be in touch.

We chose to keep Butta a secret, because he wasn't sure how they would react. I moved in with my siblings soon after. Even then I still never mentioned our other brother.

BUTTA

Sitting back and watching my siblings grow was hard but I didn't want to ruffle any feathers by adding me to the mix. I just waited until the right time.

It didn't really bother me until the day I came home and found my mother dead in the tub. It really rocked my world, both my parents dead within a month of each other. Then when I realized she killed herself I was pissed.

My mother took her own life because my father was gone. He was the only man she ever wanted and could never keep. After he passed a few more secrets were revealed and I guess that is what sent her over the edge.

The great Charles Brown had been married all these years and she just couldn't handle that. He had California in an uproar. Women from all over loved my dad and I wondered were there anymore kids going to pop up.

****

Pepper had gotten in real good, and I was happy for her. I wanted that for myself but now the time had passed and honestly I'm not sure how Carlos would respond.

I knew they might get suspicious of Pepper soon, because she does disappear a lot to chill with me. I was in a place where I just wanted my family. My aunt moved in to my mom house to help but she couldn't keep up with the payments so the house was foreclosed.

I only had a couple more months before the bank put the padlocks on the doors. Pepper had no clue because I just kept all that information to myself. I continued living my life normally; hell my aunt was actually in a convalescent home now.

My dad taught me how to survive and I damn sure wasn't going to complain about my situation. I did what I had to do to survive.

CHOCOLATE

I was really happy having a sister, especially since Charmaine proved to be a hoe and not my friend. Pepper and I had a bond instantly and it was nothing like what I went through with Charmaine. She was my sister through thick and thin and we would never turn on each other.

We had started doing everything together, besides when she made her private runs. I wasn't going to question her about her whereabouts consistently, but I was getting nosey.

"Bitch where are you always going?" I asked.

"To mind my damn business," she replied.

"Yeah whatever," I replied.

I wasn't going to push the issue; I just said fuck it and let it go. She would have given me a lame excuse anyways. I rolled me a blunt and popped in Boyz N Da Hood. I knew when Los heard the movie or smelled the trees he would join me soon.

"What you doing?" he asked as he came in.

"Watching TV," I giggled as I passed him the blunt.

"What's funny?"

"How predictable you are."

He mushed me in my face and laughed. That's all he could do because he knew it was true. We had been sitting there for about an hour before there was a knock on the door.

I looked at Carlos and he looked at me. We both were too lazy to get up, and he knew I wasn't getting up. Carlos gave me a crazy look then got up to go to the door. He opened the door and sneered his lip.

"What do you want Kwinn?" he asked.

Now I didn't know Kwinn, but I had heard about her. She was this chick from the neighborhood he grew up in. She always wanted to be with my brother but he didn't give her any play.

Kwinn was Asian and Black, but she was raised by her Asian mother. You could barely tell she had Black in her, but when she opened her mouth she was every stereotype you could think of.

"Nigga why you ain't answering my calls," she spat.

"Girl you better gon' about your business. What the fuck you doing coming around here?" he asked.

"If you answered your phone, I wouldn't have to act like a stalker."

In efforts to stifle my laughter, I inhaled quickly causing the smoke from the blunt to choke me. Carlos stepped back and glanced at me, I gave him the thumbs up to signal I was good.

"Um who the fuck is in there?" she questioned.

"None of your damn business," he replied.

"That was a bitch. I know a females cough when I hear one," she stated.

"You dumb. First off you are not my woman and never will be. Second it is a female in here and she is my sister, not that I have to explain anything to you," he informed.

"Ha! Negro when you get a sister. Don't have me fuck whatever bitch you have in there up," she threatened.

I kindly stood up and walked to the front door. Apparently this hoe had lost her mind. When I got to the door I passed the blunt to my brother then kissed him on the cheek. The bitch had the nerve to smack her thin ass lips.

"You are more than welcome to come in and join us. You smoke?" I smiled.

She frowned but welcomed the invitation to come in. As soon as she came in I closed the front door and locked it. I got reacquainted with my seat and rolled another blunt.

Once it was sparked I took a short pull and passed it to Kwinn. She looked at me strange yet smoked my weed.

"Who are you to Carlos?" she asked me.

"I'm his sister," I smiled.

Carlos was watching my every move; he didn't know what the hell was going on in my head. All I did was give him a wink and a smile. He was clueless and it was obvious.

"You must be a dumb bitch. How many bitches pretend to be the sister? That's some side bitch shit," she scoffed.

"Girl you are a complete idiot. Why would I need to lie to you? You are not his woman. If you were you would know I lived here, with my brother. I only invited you in to check your ass."

"Bitch I'm uncheckable!"

"No sweetheart you can and will be checked," I stated standing up and getting in her face.

"Carlos you better get your fake sister, with her charcoal black ass," she smirked.

If you didn't know I went through a period in my life where I was ridiculed for my chocolate skin and didn't take to kindly to dark jokes.

Before I knew I had kneed her in the stomach, and followed that with a combo set of punches and jabs.

"These charcoal fist fucking you up huh bitch?" I ranted.

Carlos sat back and allowed me to beat that bitch ass. I whooped her for her rude comments and for harassing my brother. I was over her bullshit. Part of me wanted to cut her stomach out and feed it to her, she was really lucky Carlos broke it up.

"I'm calling the police and pressing charges bitch," she huffed.

I smacked the shit out of her with my flip flops. I never used to be a fighter, but linking up with my siblings sparked something in me that I could barely contain.

"Who are you going to call?" I asked.

"Nobody?" she cried.

"Are you going to harass my brother anymore?" I asked.

She shook her head no. Pepper returned home soon after, and Kwinn looked even more confused when my sister walked in wearing my face.

"What the hell going on here? I need to fuck this bitch up?" Pepper wondered.

Pepper had no clue what was going on but she could tell Kwinn had felt my wrath, and all she wanted to know was did I need her assistance. I shook my head no, because this bitch was pathetic.

"Another sister?" she said while shaking her head.

"Yep and if you call the police I'll hunt you down and kill you while they have my sister in jail for assault," Pepper barked.

"Understood?" Carlos added.

"Understood," she answered.

With that we let her gather her things and get the hell on. Part of me felt we shouldn't let her walk out the door, but Los was cool with it.

BUTTA

I had been in the shadows for a while. My grandmother had been ill for quite some time. Since Pepper's friend was the caregiver I was able to spend time with my granny when they weren't around. I had actually been staying there and fucking the shit out of granny's caregiver Shayla.

Shayla was having a party soon and they all were attending and I planned on attending in the shadows. My sisters had some dudes they were messing with. I have yet to surveillance them since I've been at my grandmother's house stuck in Shayla's pussy.

Shayla assumed I just loved being around her; reality was I was homeless.

I had slapped every nigga in the hood so no one extended their home to me.

It was getting to the point that I was tired of being the left out sibling. Pepper begged me to just wait; she wanted the time to be right. It had been damn near a year and I was still waiting.

I called my sister and asked her to come over but she said there was a situation at the house. That's another thing; she doesn't spend the same amount of time with me, because she is always bonding with Chocolate and Carlos.

I decided to just walk the neighborhood and see what was cracking. It was silent for the most part, so I decided to spark up. I had freaked a Black & Mild; that was when u emptied a cigar without splitting it and packed it with marijuana instead of rolling a blunt.

As I walked down the Boulevard I noticed this dude coming my way but I didn't pay him any mind. I was getting high in my own little world. I crossed over to the park so I could chill and smoke. He went to the park too. I still didn't trip. Then he came towards me; I had this habit of twirling a razor under my tongue and I knew how to use my blade.

"What's up with you homie?" he said.

"Chilling," I twirled my razor.

"Let me hit something?" he asked.

Now normally weed was universal, and if you were smoking you usually shared, but I didn't feel this nigga like that.

"Nawl my nigga, I'm good," I stated.

"A nigga can't hit the weed?" he asked.

"Not this weed," I stated holding up my cigar.

"Give me that shit little nigga," he walked up on me.

"I'd advise you to back up," I smirked.

By now I was grinning from ear to ear. He was a little confused by my demeanor. I wouldn't let him see me sweat if he paid me to.

He tried to grab it out my hand, and I slapped that shit down. That made him a little angry. He immediately lunged at me. While he was lunging I stepped to the side and hit my blunt before I slapped the piss out of him, then it was on.

He grabbed me and put me in a headlock. I wiggled as much as I could and the moment I had a milligram of space I released my blade from my jaw, clinched my teeth and dug my face into his side.

Instantly he released me to grab his side, and I literally went in for his jugular. The blade went through smooth as butter. A huge smile swept my face as I watched his life slip away.

"See nigga, you lost your life over some weed," I said as I casually walked away.

I knew I had to go change my clothes but I wasn't sure if my siblings were stopping by the house. Once I made sure the coast was clear I went to my grandmother's house to change. Instead of lying up in Shayla's pussy, I made my way to this other bitch I was fucking with house.

PEPPER

When I got back to the house all I saw was my sister and this bitch going at it, and instantly I got heated. My daddy told me to always ride for a Brown and that's what I will do.

When my brother let the bitch go I could see Choc was just as disappointed as I was. Los told us it was for the best. So just like good little sisters, we agreed.

****

Time was passing faster than ever, and Butta was tired of being on the outside. I wanted him to be with us as well but quite frankly, I was scared. I thought Choc and Los would be pissed off at me. I really didn't want to lose their trust. Plus it wasn't the right time. I also had to tell my siblings about the letters my daddy left for us. They were definitely going to hate me.

We were preparing to go to Shayla's party. She had one of her home care assistant friends staying with Grandma since her party was tonight.

Lately we had been hanging with my brother's friends Ronnie, June, & Saniyah. The two guys were gorgeous. Choc and I had been flirting our asses off and we knew Los was fucking Saniyah. Ronnie and Saniyah were siblings and June was their cousin or at least I thought he was.

They were accompanying us to Shayla's party. Saniyah fell in line and ended up being a great addition to our circle. We were looking forward to partying with them tonight.

When we got to the party, the parking lot was crackin'. We decided to chill out outside for a while since it was the place to be. The other ladies and I wanted to walk around while the fellas leaned up against the cars.

It was a rowdy crowd and our nosey asses wanted to go see what was going on. So we went directly in the crowd to see. These fools had a damn Soul Train line going on in the parking lot.

We were enjoying the show when I noticed some fool all in my sister's ear. She was really tense, which caused Saniyah to tap me and point out a lone tear on Choc's face.

"Choc....Choc....Chocolate!" I yelled. "What is wrong with you?" I asked.

That's when I noticed this fool hand on my sister's shoulder. The fool was later identified as Choc's trifling ex Larry, who used to be Los' friend.

He saw my sister and tried to lay that sad ass baby I'm sorry bullshit, but I wasn't having it.

"Boohoo nigga. You cheated, you got beat on, now kick rocks," I fired as I started pacing around.

He tried telling me he heard about me and I should mind my business, but I nipped his comment in the bud real quick.

"You have no idea what involves me partna, last time I checked Choc is my sister and Carlos is my brother. So therefore my nig, anyone who hurts them or attempts to hurt them is an automatic enemy of mine. And you sir will feel my wrath. Heed my warnings," I spat.

I could see the shock all over his face. My sister kept pushing him away but this lame nigga was persistent. Before I knew it we were in a shouting match.

Ronnie had to be watching us because he swooped in like Choc's knight in shining armor. He tried checking Larry but apparently Larry needed his ass kicked.

Carlos noticed there was a lot of commotion in the area where Ronnie went to check on us girls. His gut must have told him to grab June and head over there. By the time he arrived he heard Ronnie telling Larry that he was his replacement. It was like the crowd knew some shit was about to go down. I mean niggas parted like the red sea.

"So we meet again?" Los stated.

It was a rhetorical question, we didn't give a damn what Larry had to say.

"You caught me off guard last time. That will not be happening this time around," replied Larry.

"Nah I caught you betraying mines and Chocolate's trust," Los added.

"Look Los, you have a right to be mad but I need to holla at Choc alone," he stated.

"Look homie, my lady has made it clear she ain't feeling you," Ronnie added.

"I've already asked you to stay out of business that doesn't include you," Larry said in frustration.

"Like I already told you, my lady is my business."

Chocolate was shocked at Ronnie's statement, but I saw the light bulbs flickering in her head. She put her arm around Ronnie's waist and he pulled her in close. I knew in my heart this would be the beginning of a new relationship for my sister.

"Aye L, I'm trying real hard to keep the peace man, you are really skating on thin ice," Los stated.

"Carlos I'm trying to be civil too. I need to speak with Choc alone. Shit real talk my nig you lucky I'm not putting one in your dome. That was some real bitch shit you pulled. You crept up on me with my pants down literally, all over some pussy," Larry stated.

"This has nothing to do with pussy. This is about you and your disrespect to me and my sister. You wanna talk about putting one to a nigga dome. Shit it ain't nothing but air and opportunity between us!" Carlos yelled.

My boys June and Ronnie nodded their head in agreement. Just like Larry, June was always packing. That was a little trait we picked up from him. So the heaters were definitely on us. I admit having our boys there did have us a little more hyper than normal. We had been drinking and smoking, so to say the least we were feeling ourselves.

"You talking a whole lot of ying yang, let's go toes my nig?" Larry said.

"I've been quiet long enough. Yes my brother whooped your ass. Deal with it. No you can't talk to me. No I do not forgive you, and no I do not want to get back with you. So if you haven't figured it out, there is no chance in hell of there ever being us again. I'm happy with my new man," Chocolate fired off.

"Do you really give up on us Choc?" he asked.

"Did you not hear that big ass speech my sister just gave you?" I intervened.

"Bitch I'm tired of your slick ass mou...." Larry tried to say.

Before he could finish his sentence I had already knocked him upside his head. He was amazed at my skill. I was a female Mike Tyson. Delivering jabs and right hooks. It was a full brawl. Larry's friends came to his aide as the Brown siblings and our friends handed Larry's crew one hell of an ass whooping.

Eventually we all heard sirens in the distance. The entire parking lot scattered. Everyone ran to their cars and got the hell out of dodge.

"Spark the blunt!" I yelled. I don't know how Carlos ended up in the car with us but he was getting a taste of how girls are loud as hell when we get together.

"Can you wait till we are on the freeway? Damn Tyson calm down," laughed Saniyah.

"It's cool Saniyah spark that shit now, anything to calm my crazy ass sister down."

"Hey Choc can you stop by Granny's house, so I can check in on the girl covering for Shayla," I requested.

"I'm not going in but I will take you," replied Choc.

"Hell, I don't want to go at all. Y'all know I don't be going over there," protested Carlos.

True Choc and Los loved our grandmother, but there was still animosity in their hearts. The only difference was, Choc attempted to get over it.

"You two need to stop being so cold hearted, granny really misses you both," I said.

"Well I don't know about Carlos, but I'm still healing," laughed Choc.

She could barely get that lie out of her mouth. We all knew she was laying it on thick with that corny ass line.

Carlos was in the backseat with Saniyah, who appeared to be blowed as fuck, this chick was all over him and he loved it. It hadn't even bothered me that we had just pulled up in front of my grandmother's house.

"Hurry up Pep, I don't want to be sitting out here all night," yelled Chocolate.

"Okay dang, you should just come in," I yelled back. They both ignored me and continued smoking the blunt.

After about ten long minutes I finally came out, and we headed back to our house where I'm sure June and Ronnie has been waiting.

PEPPER

Damn! Last night was something else. We were enjoying ourselves until my sister's ex came and fucked it up. I see both Charmaine and Larry becoming a problem. They can't take no for an answer, but I got a surprise for their asses. I picked up the phone and dialed a number.

"Hey, how's one of my favorite people?" I asked into the phone receiver.

"I'm all good, just tired of waiting on you. Is it time yet?" the person asked me.

"No not yet, but there is some business that needs to be handled," I replied.

"What kind of business?" he asked.

"Extermination!" was all I needed to say.

"Meet me at the house," was his request as he gave me the dial tone.

You see me and my siblings are a lot alike. Unfortunately I'm not sure if they will be willing to go as far as me. Only time will tell. Plus with all the secrets I'm harboring, they really might turn on me. I know this sounds juvenile, but I like the whole big family thing. Daddy kept us all separate long enough.

"What's up sis? Who were you on the phone with?" quizzed Chocolate.

"Why? Nosey ass," I asked.

"For that exact same reason, I'm nosey. We got bugs?" Choc replied.

"Why in the hell are you asking me about bugs?" I wondered.

"You called the exterminator right?" she asked.

"Damn! No I didn't nosey ass, you always listening to my conversations," I scoffed.

We continued to go this route as I continued to avoid her question. Eventually she got the hint and headed to her own damn room. I quickly changed clothes and headed to meet my favorite person.

BUTTA

When Pep called me about my siblings having a little problem I was all for getting down and dirty. Whether I knew them personally or not, I knew they were my sister and brother so their problems automatically became mines.

There was no wasting time in my eyes, it was now or never. Pepper and I crept up on Charmaine and fucked her up, leaving her unconscious as we drug her ass to Larry's house.

When Larry came home that night he was oblivious to what was going on inside his home. He opened the door and rushed to cut the alarm off. He continued smoking his blunt and proceeded to the kitchen. It was then when he finally felt the presence behind him. He went to reach for his gun, but a large object connected with his skull, as his world went dark.

When we woke him up he was shocked to see Pepper standing in front of him. The look on his face was pure comedic.

"Happy to see me?" she questioned.

"What the fuck is going on? Bitch, untie me," Larry cried.

He tried threatening Pepper but my fist met his face. He needed to be taught a lesson about disrespecting both my sisters. Larry fixed his mouth to question me, but Charmaine's soft whimpers stopped him in his tracks.

"Well, well, well. Look who decided to join the party," I stated.

Charmaine cried out once she noticed Larry's voice. Her eyes were swollen shut and she had on a blindfold. When I snatched the blind fold off she shrieked at the slight sight of Pepper.

I went into to the kitchen to grab my duffle bag full of tools and chemicals. I handed it to my little sister and she dug through the bag.

"I don't know why you always need this bullshit, all I need is this right here," I flicked my blade.

Pepper shook her head at me before she spoke, "You and that damn razor."

Larry and Charmaine talked amongst themselves, hoping to get away, but that wasn't going to happen. Pepper walked towards Larry and unzipped his pants. She pulled out that nigga dick and I was confused.

Pepper grabbed a rope and tied a noose around Larry's manhood with a huge smile on her face. Right as she was about to do god knows what, we heard a noise in the back. We both grabbed a weapon before we went to check it out.

It was two people outside the door, and they had a key to enter. As they pushed the door open I yelled, "Put the fucking gun down!"

The man in the ski mask replied, "What the fuck!"

The second person in the ski mask turned around and gasped.

"Brother?" Pepper asked.

The two ski masked people were Chocolate and Carlos. For the first time ever I stood face to face with all my siblings. Shit was definitely getting real, because Carlos wanted to know who I was and reality was we all looked like each other.

When Pepper confessed that I was their brother, I could see anger rising. Pepper begged them not to be angry and promised she had a good explanation. Carlos didn't want to wait till later so Pepper had no choice but to give him the shortened version.

We eliminated them in the worse possible ways, but it was great to see we were all pretty much alike. I felt good killing as a unit and watching Charmaine and Larry beg for their lives.

Pepper even admitted to holding out information from me too. Apparently my dad wrote us all letters that she has been holding on to for more than a year.

I went back to Carlos house with them, and he gave me some clothes to put on after I got out of the shower. We sat up smoked and got to know each other. It was obvious Carlos was a little bothered that our dad sent me to school for special ops training and not him.

It was amazing because we all didn't grow up too far from each other. I can't believe my dad got away with this shit so long.

Once we got over all the amazement we wanted Pepper to give us the letters she had been holding, and to think she never even read hers.

She went to her room and came back with four sealed white envelopes. Carlos' attitude was blaring now, so Choc chose to read hers out loud. We quickly realized each letter was exactly the same.

"Dear Children," she read as we all took a deep breath before she continued. *"I am writing this letter to my children. Yes I said children. In my mind I have been a great father to you all. I may not have been a hundred percent honest or faithful to your mothers but I was good to each one of you. I lived multiple lives but you never suffered for it. Hell, you all were pretty much grown before you had a clue about my infidelities. I was young and dumb back then, and trust me I am paying for it. Cancer must have been God's way of telling me I ain't right.*

Chocolate I am extremely sorry I let you down baby-girl. I know you thought you were the only one. I am truly sorry. Pepper I'm sorry I wasn't there full time, especially after your mother passed, but I am grateful for your Aunt for taking great care of you. Carlos you are definitely your father's child. I wouldn't speak to me either. It's funny how the same attitude I wore for a lifetime came back to bite me in the ass. Your response is exactly what I thought it would be. And Butta, I thank you for not hating me for not being there for you a hundred percent. I hope the CSI classes paid off. If you are anything like me, which you ALL are, I hope you are using it wisely and remember no slip ups.

That statement alone made us all look at each other. Was our dad really as sick as us? It would make sense. That would explain how we all shared the same twisted thoughts. The siblings really were paying attention now.

Well if you are reading this that means the good Lord has called me home. I am no longer there to right my wrongs. Whether you believe me or not, I loved each one of your mother's. But I made a promise to MaryAnn and I kept that promise as long as she allowed me. I promised to never leave her just like I promised my other children's mothers that I would be a father every day of the year. Do you know how hard it was working six days a week and visiting three houses and making it home to the fourth on time? No I'm not looking for your sympathy but I wanted you to know the lengths I went through for you all to be happy. Trust me if I was honest to your mother's you wouldn't be together now and cancer wouldn't have killed me but MaryAnn would have.

You guys are family and I taught you family always rides for family. Now do me proud and take care of your siblings and get to know them. Here are your names in order Carlos Brown, Butta Brown, Chocolate Brown, and Pepper Brown. I love you all and see you on the other side.

Your dad, Charles

Tears had streaked all our faces after hearing the letter. Our dad went through the extremes to keep us and all our moms happy, and to me that was amazing.

We talked about our dad and our connection a little while longer. I knew Carlos feelings were changing, because he was concerned about my living arrangements. They all thought I was living with my aunt but you already know that's a lie.

"Aye lil bro, you know there is a room for you here, right?" Carlos asked.

"I assumed it was, but I wasn't going to invite myself in," I smirked.

He let me know whenever I was ready the door was open. He didn't have to tell me twice, first thing I'm doing tomorrow was getting my things. At that moment I finally confessed that I was actually homeless.

Carlos welcomed me with open arms. For the first time ever it was the Brown siblings and we were about to celebrate. We threw some meat on the grill and made some sides. We enjoyed each other's company until we passed out.

CARLOS

I had just gotten out the shower when I heard the bamming on the door. I wasn't in a rush because I knew my little brother could handle things.

I took my time getting dressed and puffed on a blunt that was in the ashtray. When I finally made my way into the living room the homies June, Ronnie and Saniyah with her gorgeous ass, was in there. Somehow they knew Butta.

I was grateful they knew each other and got along because that would have been the end of mines, June and Ronnie's friendship if they had beef with my little brother.

Y'all know I grow instantly protective of my siblings. Once I know we share the same bloodline I instantly get protective.

I could see hanging with them was going to be pretty wild. They filled me in on how they knew one another and all I could think was this is a small world.

The girls went off to gossip and we chilled and played a few video games and put some Chronic in the air. Ronnie always came bearing herbal gifts.

BUTTA

Life was good since I moved in with my siblings. It was as if I belonged to something. I always had my mom and dad but this bond we have is totally different. I truly loved my siblings as if we grew up together.

I was sitting back on the couch listening to Al Green when my pager vibrated. I glanced down and saw that familiar area code and smiled. Leaning over I grabbed the phone off the table, and dialed the number.

"What's up my nig?" I said.

"What's up youngsta?" he replied.

"Shit just living," I replied.

"I need to holla at your pops," he requested.

"Damn my nigga, I'm sorry I didn't call but my dad passed away about a year ago."

"What?"

"Yeah I had so much going on with my siblings that I just didn't think to call."

"Oh so you know about all your siblings?"

"Yeah we met. Wait a minute; you knew?"

"Come on nigga I ain't no better and birds of a feather flock together," Nico laughed before we ended our call.

I had known Nico since I was about twelve or thirteen. He was my dad's Chicago connect. My dad used to serve a little powder and other things.

One year shit was real tough and my dad sent me to make the drop.

When I arrived in Chicago needless to say Nico was floored to see my young ass coming in making boss moves. I remember that shit like yesterday.

"I know damn well Charlie didn't send a kid to make the drop," Nico laughed.

"Fuck you!" I spat.

Nico and his crew fell out laughing. They laughed like I was a joke or something. Nico walked over to me and shook my hand.

"You got heart huh lil nigga?"

"Who the fuck is this clown?" I asked.

"I'm dat nigga!"

I laughed at him just like he did me. I wanted that nigga to feel just as small as I did. He was supposed to be the infamous Nico and here he was joking around when I was there on business.

"Can we get down to business?" I said.

"Straight business no play, lil man? I like that," he smirked.

"Yeah whatever nigga," I mean mugged.

He emptied the room and wanted to talk to me alone. I wasn't scared at all; something in me said I wish this nigga would. He was impressed by my lack of fear.

"My dad sent me to handle this lil business."

"I swear you lil Charles all day," Nico laughed.

I wasn't for that laughing shit. I cocked my hand back as far as it would go and slapped the shit out of Nico. It was obvious he was pissed and wanted to take me out but I immediately was in a fighting stance.

"Yeah you Charlie little boy," he laughed as he pulled me in for an embrace.

And just like that Nico and I became the best of friends. He realized that I rode harder than most of the older niggas. My dad didn't use me for anymore drops, but Nico sent for me on a regular just to hang until he saw the killer in me, and that was all she wrote.

"Aye goofball, you hear me talking to you," Pepper pulled me out of my thoughts.

"Nah what's up?"

"Choc and I was about to leave and Carlos was M.I.A so we had to tell you," she stated.

"Where y'all going?" I asked.

"To Shoreline Village."

I didn't mind them going to Long Beach but reality was Carlos was really overprotective. I told them cool, but I paged Los just to be on the safe side. I knew that nigga was out with Ronnie and June.

I stayed my ass in the house because I was grateful to have a home. Plus I didn't want to share my brother's time. I know that's some little kid shit, but I never had a brother before.

Once the girls left I rolled me a blunt and got comfortable. I turned to the Cartoon Network and made me a huge bowl of cereal. It was about to go down. Tom & Jerry were up to their crazy antics.

It hadn't been one full hour since Pepper and Chocolate left and the weed was settling in my system. I leaned back to get comfortable and grabbed my meat; not on some freaky shit just sitting comfortable, when my pager beeped. I didn't recognize the number but I called anyways.

"Anybody page Butta?"

"My nigga both your sisters are about to get into some bullshit," the caller stated.

"Rick?"

"Yeah nigga. You might want to hurry up," Rick stated.

"Where y'all at? Shoreline?"

"Nope Houghton Park."

Those damn girls always went somewhere other than what they said. I snatched my keys off the table and jumped in my ride. I was smashing on the 91 freeway, all the way to the Atlantic Avenue. exit.

When I arrived at the park there was a crowd near the side fence of Jordan High. I knew instantly that's where my sisters were. As I jumped out my car with my blade under my tongue and a silver metal bat in my hand I was ready for war.

"Pep…..Choc!" I yelled.

The crowd parted as I entered with a look of fury on my face. Pepper was standing face to face with some nigga and Choc was in a fighting stance. I asked no questions, I called for my sisters to back up and I got to swinging.

Whoever that nigga was just learned a valuable lesson; don't fuck with my sisters. The crowd dispersed and only left a few looky lou's behind.

I didn't bother with killing the dude; we just got the hell out of dodge. I made there drama prone asses come home. They were mad but I didn't give a fuck.

When we arrived at the house Los was there alone, and I was actually grateful. My adrenaline was running and I wanted to beat a few more niggas.

"What the fuck happened? Why are you covered in blood?" Carlos questioned me.

"I had to get this nigga off my sisters."

I saw his face frown and turn towards the girls, who was now looking at the floor. They knew he was about to get in their asses.

"Where did y'all go?"

"They told me Shoreline," I snitched.

"So where did he find y'all?"

"Houghton Park," mumbled Choc.

"Excuse me?"

"Houghton Park," she spoke a little louder.

"FUCK!"

CARLOS

I clearly told my sisters not to go to that park, due to the fact I was beefing with some niggas over that way. I knew how niggas got down and if they couldn't get me, then they had to get to me by going through my family.

In order to not knock both my sisters the fuck out, I punched a hole in the hall door. I was so pissed and didn't know where to direct my anger.

"You kill him?"

"No," replied Butta

The frustrations sat in my head and I found myself chain smoking on Chronic. I didn't want to be bothered with no one, but my brother followed me to my room.

"You good?" he asked me.

"Nawl I'm heated."

"I sent that nigga a real good message," Butta stated.

"Yeah but now we have to worry about them retaliating."

"We could go take him and his crew out," my little brother smiled wide.

I was all for his last suggestion and wanted to move quickly. I knew dude that he beat with the bat was hospitalized, but his homeboys had to want it.

I wasn't one for waiting too long and over strategizing, so that night I drugged my sisters. I know it sounds bad but I did. I laced their hyper active asses, drinks with Benadryl, so they were out like a light.

Butta and I crept out the house and got a getaway car. We drove to the Norf side of Long Beach while puffing on a blunt and listening to Pac. Just like I thought those fools were posted in the back of the park getting high.

"There them niggas go," I pointed towards them.

Butta hit the lights on the car, cutting them off. He pulled over and killed the engine. I took a deep pull of the blunt to make sure my mind was right.

"It's about five of them," Butta stated.

"You scared?" I glanced at him.

"Fuck you," he frowned.

I laughed at his silly ass, and we exited the car. We both had metal bats tonight. We were beast with blades and knives but we weren't damn fools.

We didn't walk up talking all kind of shit, we walked up swinging. We were busting heads wide the fuck open. The last two we hit a few times but the urge to slice a nigga took over.

I flicked my knife and stuck him in his chest, while Butta freed his blade from his mouth. We were in real killer mode now. These niggas should be asking the creator to forgive them for their sins.

"Aaaaaaggghhhh!" one guy yelled.

"Take it like a man," I uttered.

"It wasn't me," the other confessed.

"But you hang with him," Butta replied.

Since they were yelling and begging like bitches we decided to just put them out of their misery and get ghost. We hopped on the freeway and raced towards our home, not before stopping off and ditching the car.

My brother had his car parked not too far from where we ditched the getaway car. His seats were covered in plastic just in case we had any blood splatter on us. I had to admit I was jealous my dad trained Butta for shit like this and not me.

"We did that shit," he boasted.

"Hell yeah, bustin' heads open."

"And pulling out throats."

We were so amped up we were hoping anyone else wanted the drama we brought. The Brown brothers were ready to wreak all kinds of havoc.

We bypassed our house and was cruising while smoking in a low frequency area. Life was good. We changed into some basketball shorts he had in the back and bagged our other clothes and put them in the trunk. Flashing lights and the sounds of sirens stopped us in our tracks.

"Here we go with this shit," I stated.

"Well, well, well, Butta Brown," the Highway patrol stated.

"Eric Jackson," Butta laughed.

"That's Officer Jackson now," he corrected.

"Well how may I help you today, Officer Jackson?" he smirked.

Eric and my dad went way back to sandbox days. They weren't the best of friends and Butta may have slapped the shit out of his kids once or twice, so this could go good or bad.

"Did you know your tail light was out?" Officer Jackson asked.

"No I didn't but I'll get it taken care of first thing in the morning."

"What's that I smell? A little marijuana, huh?" he flashed his flashlight in the car.

Butta looked at me and tucked the bag of weed under his seat. I knew just by the conversation Eric wasn't in a friendly mode.

"Don't move! What you got in your hand?" he yelled.

Butta paused and we locked eyes. Apparently Officer Jackson wanted problems; he had no idea what he was asking for.

"Step out the car slowly one at a time with your hands on your head; the driver will go first," he ordered.

"Eric is this necessary?" I smiled.

"That's Officer Jackson, now out of the car pretty boy," he barked.

Butta and I followed his instructions. We both noticed he hadn't called any back-up. He pulled my wallet out as my brother sat on the ground.

"Carlos Brown?" You related to this son of a bitch?" he asked while pointing at Butta.

"He's my little brother," I frowned.

"Well hot damn, another one of Charles Brown's spawns. I swear I hated your old man. I wasn't even a bit sad when they told me he died either," he chuckled.

"What the fuck you say?" I wondered.

Before he could reply I had turned around and cracked him in his jaw. As he stumbled back, Butta jumped to his feet like a cat and rocked his other side.

"You couldn't leave well enough alone, could you?" I stated.

Before he could grab his gun, my brother slit his wrist. Reaching down to grab his wrist he caught my shank to his ear. I pulled my bloody knife out of his ear and stabbed his jaw.

"It's like butter baby," my brother yelled as he slit his throat.

Here we were again bloody and a mess. There was no doubt we needed to get home, but before we left my brother cleaned the scene to the best of his abilities.

PEPPER

I woke up in the middle of the night groggy as hell. It took me some time to get my thoughts together, and the last thing I remember was chilling with my family.

My sister was sleep and there was no sign of my brothers anywhere. I walked to the kitchen and got me a glass of water. On the way to the kitchen I discovered half of a blunt in the ashtray.

"Hell yeah, let me hit this shit," I spoke out loud.

After sparking up I finally got my glass of water. I sat back on the couch to get comfortable. I had only taken two good hits before my sister waltzed her pothead ass in here.

"Puff, puff, pass bitch," she stated.

"Damn bitch did you smell it in your sleep?" I asked.

"Shut up. My heads real cloudy, I had to have been super tired," she confessed.

"Me too because I felt foggy waking up."

My sister and I couldn't fathom why we felt that way and pushed the thoughts to the back of our head. We decided to make us a late night weed head meal.

"I'm hungry as fuck," I said.

"Me too," she replied.

"What you want?" I wondered.

We went back and forth, but honestly couldn't choose because we wanted everything. After looking through the refrigerator and cabinets multiple times we settled on Pastrami Chili Cheese fries.

She threw us a couple of Mango Madness Snapple's in the freezer and rolled a blunt as I peeled potatoes. We prepared our meal listening to Shai's tape.

"Bitch this shit is good," I mumbled through chews.

"Hell yeah," she replied.

While we were eating we saw headlights and moments later our brothers entered the house. I knew instantly they had handled someone.

They both had a happy glazed look on their faces. It was either death or getting some pussy and in my opinion that look spelled murder.

"Where y'all been?" Chocolate immediately asked.

"What y'all doing up?" Los asked.

"I asked first," Choc stated.

"And I said answer my question," he barked.

She furrowed her brows but answered his question. Then they filled us in on what sounds like the most exciting night in Brown history.

"We a team, you can't handle shit and leave us out," I protested.

"I didn't need y'all there for this," Carlos informed.

I was pissed off because he got mad whenever we did shit without them, but they feel like they could get it in without us. I was heated inside but not dumb enough to voice it.

The four of us went back and forth on what a team meant; while we smoked of course. I really enjoyed having siblings, it was a beautiful thing. Then out of nowhere the doorbell rings.

Los walked to the door and peeked out the peephole. He looked at me, and then shook his head.

"What the fuck?" he mumbled while opening the door.

"Hey fambam what's popping?" Malina stated while walking in.

"Lina?" I spoke.

Malina was our cousin but my family was extremely estranged. Hell you see I just met my siblings. She didn't live too far but we all rarely fucked with each other. Lina was a year or two older than Los and Butta.

"In the flesh," she boasted.

"What the fuck are you doing over here in the middle of the night?" Los asked.

"I got into it with my fiancé and didn't want to drive home. You know my fiancé live not too far from here," she kept talking.

She kept throwing the word fiancé around like we gave a shit. That girl must have lost her mind. Popping up around here like she talks to us on a regular; honestly I didn't know her.

"Sorry about y'all daddy, I been meaning to come around here," she stated.

"Sure you have," I said.

"Oh you look just like Choc. These Brown genes are strong," she smiled.

Chocolate introduced us and I was shocked to discover she already knew Butta. I immediately felt left out like my dad didn't want me to know my own family.

"I missed y'all; pass the blunt nigga," she continued talking.

This girl was talking a mile a minute and I couldn't keep up. Once the weed got into her system she slowed down some and I was grateful.

"Who is this nigga you supposed to be marrying?" Butta asked.

"His name is Randy and he is the sweetest man I have ever met. He respects me and would whoop a nigga ass for disrespecting me," she bragged.

"Where he from?" Los asked.

"Damn he from Compton but don't technically bang."

"Hmmmm, hmmmm," I added.

She talked about Randy non-stop he was the bee's knees apparently. We talked until everyone literally passed out.

CHOCOLATE

I was shocked to wake up and still see Malina here. I couldn't believe she popped up in the middle of the night after us not seeing her for a couple years.

"Rise and shine sunshine," I sang.

"What time is it?" she asked.

"Almost 1:00 pm."

"DAMN!"

She started scrambling around like she was crazy and moving real fast. I had to pause and make sure we only gave the bitch weed; she was acting real suspect.

"You okay?"

"Girl I have to meet Randy in a half an hour."

I looked at her like she was crazy, I could have sworn she said they got into it, but oh well not my problem.

I helped her gather her belongings and just like that our blast from the past was again past.

Since my siblings were still in their rooms I hopped in the shower in efforts to get my day started. I knew I wanted to go to the mall today, so I had to get real cute.

As I put my final touches on, my siblings all started to emerge from their rooms. Pepper gave me a funny look then flicked me off.

"Hoe, where you going?"

"To the mall."

"You couldn't wake me? I like the mall too."

"Well hurry up and get dressed."

She was talking major shit while she got her clothes together and prepared for her shower. I shrugged that shit off because I was about to wake and bake.

My brothers smelled the weed and came running. I knew I couldn't take one to the head living with three other weed heads. I immediately obliged and passed the blunt.

****

So much had been going on in our lives that I honestly didn't know what to do. I had found out that my entire life I was lied to. I went from being an only child to being a little sister and a big sister all in a year's time; my life was fucked up.

Pepper and I walked through the mall stopping in every shoe store we saw. There wasn't really anything we were there for but if we saw it we bought it. Carlos kept us living just as comfortable as my dad did when he was living.

I'm not sure how much the insurance policies were but Carlos continues to keep us living that life of luxury. He is even forcing me and Pepper to enroll back in school.

We both want to graduate so we are definitely headed back to school soon. He said he wasn't going to tolerate us getting a GED. He said we are

Browns and Browns get Diplomas. So therefore back to school we go.

BUTTA

I was annoyed with my cousin popping up, nine times out of ten that bitch was on some bullshit. She always had me fixing her bullshit. She stayed in drama and this Randy nigga sound too good to be true.

When I woke up and seen she was gone I was happy as hell, I didn't feel like dealing with any bull she brought with her.

Since my sisters were gone I asked Carlos to go play some ball with me. We made our way to the gym and you know us we were side tracked by bitches.

We saw a couple females I knew from back in the day and those hoes were looking good as fuck. I swooped in on them coming out the store, all you saw was ass and titties.

"Yo Nisha what's up?" I yelled.

"Oh shit, let me hear it one time."

"It's like butter baby," I laughed.

That was my line and for some reason the bitches loved hearing it. Her and her homegirl Leah walked up to my car. They were thick as fuck.

"Where you been lately?" Leah asked.

"I moved; I live with my brother and sisters now."

They leaned in to get a good look at Carlos. I saw a smile creep across their face. I knew they thought my brother looked good, shit we had the same features.

"What y'all about to get into?" Nisha asked.

"Y'all!" Carlos replied.

"Is that so?" Leah asked.

"That's real shit," I added.

My brother got out the car and opened the backdoor for the ladies. I ran into the store and bought a bottle of Christian Bros and a few more blunts. We were headed to a motel to fuck these bitches.

"Are we going back to your house?" Nisha wondered.

"Nope to the momo," I answered.

These bitches wasn't about to know where I laid my head, we were about to smash these bitches then drop them off.

When we arrived at the motel on Long Beach Blvd., I paid but had the girls put the room in their names. We were in the room with smoke filling our lungs and liquor going through our veins.

"We appreciate the smoke and the drinks, but what y'all working with?" asked Nisha.

"Let's get it crackin' then," Los smiled.

They both dropped down to their knees and pulled out our dicks and put them in their mouths. These bitches must do this on a regular, because they synchronized sucked our shit.

When they thought we were about to bust one, the bitches switched dicks. I looked at my brother and he was already looking at me. We both looked down at those broads and gave each other a pound on the fist. This was some real pimp shit.

Then the craziest shit happened the hoes pushed us both down on the bed. I went to grab a condom off of the table. I definitely wasn't hittin' that bitch raw, but the bitch tried to hit me in the head with the bottle of liquor instead.

Then it dawned on me, these bitches were going to rob us; hell yeah they had done this shit before. We walked right into two bored bitches looking for a come up.

"Bitch what the fuck you think you doing?" I asked as I punched her in the face.

Immediately my brother followed suit. Once we had put them bitches to sleep, we discussed if they should be put to sleep permanently.

"At least we got some head," Los joked.

"You stupid my nigga," I laughed.

"Shit I'm serious; what you want to do with these simple bitches? I mean they are your friends?" he smirked.

"I don't give a fuck; we can dead these tricks."

I walked over to Nisha and kicked her over onto her back. I wanted to dead the bitches but reality set in and my nut was in her mouth.

"We can't, our nut is in these bitches mouths."

"Damn! It's cool let's go."

I knew my brother must have had a plan because he grabbed his shit, fixed his clothes and smoothly walked out. That nigga was cool then a muthafucka.

We went directly home and he hadn't mentioned it or said anything, he was just riding and smoking. Once he got in the house he still didn't say much about it but however he was conversing with me.

My sisters walked their ass in with literally one bag each. They were gone all day but came home with one bag.

"I thought y'all had bought the mall," I laughed.

"No we actually tried on everything in the mall, but only wanted these shoes," Pepper replied.

I laughed and told my sisters about mines and Los' day. Both of my sisters were mad but Pepper knew both Leah and Nisha; needless to say she was pissed.

"The fuck you mean they tried to rob you?" she spat.

"Them bitches gave us head and everything," added Carlos.

"Where they at?" she wondered.

"We left them sleep on the floor at the motel," I answered.

"What motel and what room number?" Choc asked.

"They probably gone," stated Carlos.

"No those greedy hoes are there. It's a free room; y'all paid already, so

I'm positive they are there," stated Choc.

I knew what that look on my sisters faces meant. Someone was about feel their wrath. Carlos was cheesing bigger than me. Chocolate and Pepper didn't say anything they went to their rooms and came back in leggings and a tan tops.

Pepper had on her tennis shoes and Choc sat on the couch to lace hers. Once done they headed to the door.

"What motel and what room number?" Pepper asked.

Carlos answered her with no hesitation. I started walking to the door and they quickly shut my ass down.

"We got this," Choc informed.

PEPPER

I was ready to pound on these bitches. Who the fuck did they think they were? Nobody and I mean nobody put their hands on or try and set up my brothers. I would kill any nigga or bitch who tried.

"These bitches have no idea," I said.

"But they about to find out," Choc replied.

My sister and I jumped in her car and she sped to the motel Carlos informed us about. It didn't take that long to get there but my sister was speeding, so that helped.

"Park right there," I pointed to an open space right in front of the room number.

Chocolate swooped in the parking stall and hadn't even fully parked before we both were opening the doors. I wasn't in the mood to play these hoes. I didn't give a fuck about who they had in there with them, because their asses were ours.

"BOOM! BOOM! BOOM!" the door sounded.

Nisha opened the door and I punched her square in the nose. She stumbled back and Leah jumped up off the bed. Some busted ass dude came out of the bathroom in a towel.

"Oh shit I get all four for one price?" he wondered.

I pulled a knife from under my shirt. It was attached to a cute pink holster. Without hesitation it flew across the room and connected with his Adams Apple.

He fell into the wall as those two bitches tried to scream. Chocolate caught Leah by the throat and I grabbed Nisha.

"So you were going to rob my brother?" I asked.

"It was Nisha's idea," Leah squeezed out instead.

"Shut up," uttered Nisha.

Chocolate started to pound on Leah's face. They were not in no form or fashion ready for us. I stood back so Nisha could catch her breath. I could kill a nigga but I was in definite need of a fight.

We were in that motel room rumbling. I was glad they eventually started to fight back, because it would make killing them even sweeter. I drug Nisha across the room and slammed her head on the table.

I left her there to check on dude from the bathroom. His dumb ass tried pulling the knife out, and bled out. I snatched my knife and wiped his blood onto the towel. Then took the same knife and slit Nisha's throat. Chocolate had cut both Leah's wrist and ankles and allowed her to bleed out.

"Whewww I love this shit!" I stated.

"Me too but let's bounce."

We quickly rushed home and cleaned ourselves off. Butta was pissed.

Not that we killed them but we didn't tell him and allow him to make sure we left no evidence. He rushed out the door with his duffle bag in hand.

I knew he was hoping to get there and clean-up before the staff came and found the bodies. I knew he could break into any lock so I wasn't worried about him getting in the room, he would do that with ease.

"Was there anyone else there with them?" Carlos asked.

"Some lame ass dude, but we ended him immediately," I said.

"That's what's up," he stated.

Instead of smoking again like normal I decided to beat my brother in some old school Nintendo. We played for hours, Choc even joined in.

When Butta got back he cleaned himself up and went straight to the kitchen. The aroma of onions and garlic flowed through the house. I couldn't even concentrate; my stomach had begun to growl so loud.

"Damn nigga, you have a demon in there," Carlos joked while pointing at my stomach.

"Shut up! I 'm starving and smelling the food is making it worse," I laughed.

I jumped up and went into the kitchen. Butta was making spaghetti and the meat alone had me drooling. I was ready to get my grub on.

He had sauce simmering and was buttering the bread with garlic butter. He had even made a Caesar salad. I started getting plates so he could feed our greedy asses.

"What you doing?" Butta asked.

"Helping."

"Your ass must be starving because you ain't never volunteered to help," he smiled.

"You know me so well."

Before he made the plates Carlos rolled a blunt to ensure we were hungry. We were about to smash that food. The more I hit the weed the tighter the knot in my stomach became.

"Fuck this I need to eat," I blurted.

They all laughed in unison but I made my point. Butta got up and started making plates. After the meal was over I laid my ass down.

BUTTA

After I fed my family, I grabbed some weed and a few blunts. I was headed to this fine ass Dominican and black chick house I fucked with named Drea. She was sexy as fuck and I knew I wanted to bang those walls.

As soon as I got there she was in her favorite position; at her desk typing on that damn computer. She loved to write and told me she would be famous one day. She kept talking about loyalty and respect. I just laughed at her dreams; all I wanted was the pussy.

"Hello," I stated.

"Oh I didn't hear you come in; hey babe," replied Drea.

"That's all I get? I could go back home you know."

"I'm sorry," she stated as she stood and came towards me.

She had her hair pinned up in a loose bun, I gently released her hair. She looked at me crazy but she knew I loved pulling on her hair.

"I gotta finish this chapter first. Go on ahead and roll some weed," she stated.

"That chapter can wait."

"I'm almost done," she stated.

She had the sexiest voice. My dick instantly got hard. I rolled up blunts while she finished her chapter. Watching her prepare to live her dream was a huge turn on.

When she was done she saved her file and went to windows media player, and hit the play button. The music flowed through the speakers and Drea sashayed her sexy ass to me.

She grabbed my hand and led me to the chaise lounge. Drea pushed me down then began to seductively dance around.

"Fuck all that slow moving, make it clap," I stated.

Drea dropped down into a sort of frog looking squat position, and that fat ass started moving up and down, left to right and jiggled in all the right places.

I was grateful that she only had on a t-shirt and thong when I arrived. Her smooth sexy skin shined and glistened as she popped what her momma gave her.

By now, I was ready to blow her back the fuck out. I stood up while she did her thing and enticed me. I had already freed my dick and put on a rubber. Drea was bringing it back up and dropping it back low.

The next time she brought it up; my dick tapped her on the butt. She smiled and instead of all the bullshit foreplay I rammed all nine inches in.

"Damn, your pussy wet as fuck," I mumbled.

"Oooohhhh shit wait," she begged.

I was so far up inside of her that I felt her organs. Her pussy was so tight and silky that I could see myself falling in love; with her pussy that is.

I continued pounding in and out of her, and she was throwing that ass back. Drea had begun bouncing so hard on my dick I was trying not to bust. I tried thinking of everything I could as she threw that pussy at me. Finally I pulled out in effort to prevent myself from cumming.

"What the fuck Butta?"

"You trying to make a nigga cum too soon."

"You always bust more than one nut. Wait who else you been fucking today? That's the only reason you would be worried about cumming too soon," she spat.

"I ain't fuck nobody girl! Quit trippin'. I just wanted to bust one major nut, that's all."

"Hmmm, hmmm."

That girl had a smart ass mouth and was quick to tell you about yourself. Here she was copping an attitude as I watched my shit get limp.

"Stop trippin', look you killin' my shit," I stated while pointing at my dick.

She frowned at me and crossed her arms. I took the condom off and started putting my clothes back on. I knew she wasn't about to let this go, but then she fooled me.

"Negro, what the hell are you doing?"

"Getting dressed."

"Ummmm why?"

"Because you about to start trippin'."

"Did you hear me scream out 'Butta Brown'?"

"Nope," I cocked my head to the side and just stared at her.

"Then you can't leave here till I cum and scream your name.

A slight smile crept over my face as I sat down and sparked a blunt. Drea ass knew how to put a smile on my face; she dropped to her knees, pulled my dick out and took in every inch down her throat.

"Hell yeah," I moaned.

She released it out and spit on the head. When Drea started massaging it, my dick grew larger. She leaned in and took my nuts in her mouth.

I was in heaven, out of all the bitches I was fucking Drea gave the best head. This other bitch I was fucking with named Yolonda, whom I called Yolo, could suck a mean dick too. I wondered if they would consider having a threesome.

Drea stopped sucking my nuts and jumped on top of me and slid down on my dick, bringing me out of my fantasy of fucking Yolo and Drea at the same time.

"You like this pussy?"

"Yeah ma, this shit bomb."

Those very words caused Drea to start riding me hard and fast. I knew I was going to nut this time, so I grabbed her by the waist and started thrusting back at her.

"Oh shit… oh shit… B…B…B… Buuuutttttaaaaaa!" she yelled.

"Come all over my dick," I requested.

The more she came, the wetter her pussy was, and I was on the verge of blowing. I pushed her up and down then finally up off of me. She quickly bent down and put my dick in her mouth. Drea collapsed her jaws and I came all down her throat.

She continued sucking after I came, and I was literally in tears. My dick head was so sensitive at the moment that it felt so good it hurt. She finally released my dick with a smirk on her face.

"Bet you whatever other bitch you fucking can't fuck you like me."

I knew she was telling the truth, her head game was fantastic and her pussy was as tight as a virgin's pussy. The more I thought about how tight her shit was my dick started moving again.

Drea had picked up the blunt I dropped in the ashtray earlier and was sitting next to me. I leaned her back and dove in. Her pussy was still juicy from us fucking so I licked that up.

"Damn baby," she moaned as she grabbed my head and pulled me in.

I was sucking the life out of her pussy and she was screaming my name. I clamped down on her clit which caused her to start scooting away. I put my hands on her hips and held her firmly in place.

Once she started humping and grinding on my face I knew she was at her peak. She had locked her legs together around my neck, I tried coming up for air but she wasn't having it.

The only thing I could think to do was make her come faster. I was sucking and licking as if my life depended on it. The moment she came she released my neck. I could barely stand but I slid back into that pussy.

"Whose pussy is this?"

"Yours daddy yours."

I lifted both of her legs onto my shoulder, and plunged in deeper. She was sucking on my neck as I gave her this dick.

My nut was building with every pump, and I felt no need to fight it. I nudged her to lay all the way back. While I grind inside of her I took one of her smooth chocolate nipples in my mouth.

The sensation of her nipple firming up in my mouth had me ready to burst. I continued to suck her titties as I pulled out and came on her stomach. I knew we didn't use rubbers after the first mishap, but I wasn't dumb enough to cum inside her.

"Now that was good Butta, real good," she grinned.

I got dressed, kissed her on the forehead and headed out. She knew I rarely stayed long and after we were done fucking I wanted to go home, smoke a blunt then pass the fuck out.

On my way home I got a page from this other bitch named Shonda. I met her in Arkansas a few years back. After giving her some of this good dick, the bitch packed up and moved to California as soon as she finished high school. I know I gave the best dick, but that was ridiculous. I let Carlos fuck her a few times. Instead of her being done with us both, she's still fucking with me.

I ignored her calls because a nigga was worn out. I couldn't fuck another bitch today if I tried. She had some good country pussy so you now that was in my plans.

CARLOS

Shonda popped up at the house while we all were chilling, looking for Butta. He was ignoring her calls, which meant he was already up in some pussy. I had no problem with fucking this bitch.

"What you want Shonda?" I asked.

"Some dick," she answered.

"Me or my brother?"

"You," she smiled.

I took her back to my room and didn't waste any time. I remember how good her pussy was, so I was happy to oblige.

I got a condom out of my underwear drawer, and sat next to her on the bed. Shonda immediately leaned in and kissed me, she smelled good like strawberries.

I lifted her sundress over her head to admire her thick frame. It was something about a thick bitch that turned me on. I freed her breast and sucked each one diligently.

"Mmmmm Los this feels so good."

I continued to suck, and my hand found her already wet pussy. I plunged my middle finger inside her hole and she opened her legs wider. Then it hit me, this bitch didn't have on any panties. She knew exactly what she was coming for.

As my finger went in and out my thumb massaged her clit. When her clit was completely slippery, I slipped on a condom.

I sat her on top of my dresser, slightly hanging her bottom off the dresser and slid my dick in. Her pussy felt so good I instantly grew a little larger.

Her breast was in my mouth and I continued to push my dick inside of her. I leaned back a little so I could see my dick go in and out. Seeing all her juices on my dick was a huge turn on. I was fucking the hell out of her pussy and she was pumping just as hard.

I picked her up and stood in the middle of the floor pumping in and out of her. She released her hands from around my neck and bent all the way down. She is in this upside down position and I was killing the pussy.

Shonda turned around while I was fucking her, and we ended up in a doggy style position. This bitch was definitely porn material. I pulled out and eased my dick in her butt slowly. She clinched her cheeks tight and looked back.

I gave that baby relax look and pushed my love inside. After a few moments she loosened up and threw that ass at me. I continued grinding until I came and collapsed.

"That was bomb, but next time no booty love without me knowing," she stated.

I agreed, but I really didn't give a fuck, it was time for her to bounce. I tossed her dress to her and she frowned. She knew what it was. I was nice enough to walk her to the front door. Butta had just walked up the porch.

"Hey Butta," she sang.

"What up Shonda," he spoke.

He gave me a pound and keeps it moving. It was obvious she felt funny about him just walking past. He knew I had just fucked her so there was no reason for him to hang around.

"Welp can I get a kiss goodbye?"

I wasn't a big kisser, but I leaned in and gave her a peck; after all she had just hooked a nigga up. We parted ways and I headed back in the house.

CHOCOLATE

My family was full of hoes and it's my daddy's fault. He left us some major flawed genes. We are a bunch of hoes and murderers. When I saw Shonda arrive Pep and I split, we knew they were about to fuck and that damn girl got loud.

We didn't really have a destination so we just cruised and ended up wherever it took us. This particular journey took us to Bellflower. We knew a few people who lived on Cornuta.

Once we made it to Bellflower, we ended up getting sidetracked and going to the Sherwood Apt. instead. We were parking lot pimping with a few associates when some whack ass dude walked up.

"Y'all too loud," he said to the crowd.

We all burst into laughter, who did this clown think he was? Apparently that pissed him off because he started yelling obscenities and saying he would call the police, which is a huge no-no.

"Are you security?" Pepper asked.

"No I'm a paying tenant," he barked.

"Do you pay for the parking lot or your apartment?" she laughed.

"You ghetto bitches and niggas are really disrespectful."

"Excuse me?" I said.

"Bitch you heard me," he frowned.

"Wrong answer," I replied.

This black muthafucka was pretty fucking big. I know Pep and I was beast with the blades, but this was a big muthafucka. I was instantly thinking of ways to kill him.

"You know you done fucked up right?" Pepper asked.

"No you have fucked up. This is trespassing. Every month apartment 202 is paid for and I don't have to tolerate ghetto bullshit.

"Ok 202 we are so sorry," I smiled.

Pep looked in my eyes and smiled too, she knew I wasn't going to try this big muthafucka but he would get his. His big ass had no clue about them Browns but he was about to learn.

The crowd began to disperse, and we left the parking lot as well. We rode around the corner pass K-Mart and doubled back to the building. We parked on the street instead of going back to the parking lot. We knew we wanted to slip in and out.

My sister and I crept up to apartment 202 and knocked on the door. As soon as Mr. Parking Lot opened the door I stuck his ass in the throat. Pepper threw alcohol on his open wound and in his eyes.

He stumbled back trying to clinch his throat and my sister sliced his face. He looked at me with confusion and I let off a huge grin before whispering, "Next time be more respectful." His eyes rolled in the back of his head and our mission was done.

Instead of hanging out the rest of the night, it was right back home to have a concrete alibi. I knew we were there but we left just like all the other patrons. That's my story and I'm sticking to it.

BUTTA

When I noticed my sisters pulling up; I knew they had been in some shit. It was like before we all linked up we got into minor shit but as a unit, we were wreaking havoc on this world.

Chocolate and Pepper rushed out the car and to the door. I already had it open for them. They were stripping out of their clothes really fast.

"Aye Los...what did y'all do?" I said in one breath.

Carlos entered the room, and the pair started to confess. Words were flying out of their mouths. He told Chocolate to explain what the hell had happened.

"We were chilling, then this dude got real disrespectful and well a little voice said for me to gut his ass."

I was so tired of cleaning up behind my reckless sisters, it wasn't even funny. I loved when we moved as a unit and not like this. This was chaotic. They tried assuring us that they got in and got out.

I knew they were professional like me, but my gut said some shit would soon follow. After disposing of their clothes I rolled a blunt to mellow the mood.

"Roll a few more, lil bro," Carlos requested.

"Fa' sho my nig."

"We sippin' tonight?" Pepper asked.

"Nah, I'm good," I replied.

"Hmmmph," Choc pursed her lips.

It was like in order for us to drink, we all had to agree. I don't know who made that silent rule, but I was a smoker. I didn't always need a drink; all I needed was to make sure my smoke was endless.

I heard the phone ringing and jumped up to get it. I was hoping it was one of my bitches. Instead it was another familiar voice.

"What up baby boy?" Nico spoke loudly.

"What's going on Chi-town?"

"I got this new shit I want you to check out."

"Word?"

"Word!"

"Bet; send that shit."

"Already on its way."

We disconnected the call, and I let my brother know my boy Nico was sending us some fire from the Chi. I was extremely amped. He had good weed, but it wasn't like that Cali weed.

We sat blazing and enjoying each other's company. Times like this I really enjoyed having siblings. I really wish my dad wouldn't have kept us apart.

The next morning this chick I met from Connecticut named Shaniqua popped up at my house. She had been in town visiting her family and just like all the bitches I came across she wanted a piece of me.

"What you doing here?" I asked.

She didn't respond, instead she burst into tears. I barely knew this broad and she came here crying. I could fuck her but being sympathetic was a stretch.

"You are the only person I know out here and someone killed my uncle," she cried.

I looked down at her confused then decided to embrace her and let her cry. Then it dawned on me to ask my sisters where in the hell were they last night.

Pepper entered the room with a confused look on her face. She had never met Shaniqua before, and never really seen me compassionate to anyone but my siblings.

"Ummmm, what the hell going on here?"

"The home-girl uncle got killed."

"A lot of that going around," Pepper casually spoke.

She proceeded to the kitchen to grab a quick snack. On her way out Choc was also entering the living room. Shaniqua had finally lifted her head. I could tell she was kind of embarrassed by her actions.

"You good lil mama?"

"I'm straight I just need to contact my family so I can know what to do."

I sat her down and decided to get her a bottle of water. When I came back she had her screw face on. I had no clue what happened in between me going to the kitchen and back.

"What's up?" I wondered.

"I think your sisters killed my uncle."

Immediately the dynamics of the room changed. My stance became defensive and Pepper darted to the door and locked it.

"Code Red!" Pep yelled out.

Carlos came rushing to the room while Choc closed all the blinds. Shaniqua stood there wondering what moves to make. Tears flooded her face as a smile crept over mines.

"I should just go," Shaniqua stated.

We never liked handling anything in our house and I felt kind of bad for her. She had good pussy and it seems that I always had to kill the ones with that good snatch.

Choc shoved her on the couch as Pepper went through her purse. She went for her phone and her wallet. I immediately knew where she was going with her search. Carlos snatched the items from her and looked through them before speaking.

"The Morgan family will be pretty upset if you don't return to Connecticut," Carlos stated.

Shaniqua knew exactly what my brother meant, and began crying hysterically. Witness wasn't something we usually left but some circumstances we could just pump fear in their hearts and they would fall in line.

"Are y'all going to kill me too?" she cried.

"Do we need to?" I asked.

"No sir! I'm heading back to Connecticut today," she assured me.

I copied her ID information down and Pep snapped a picture of her for reference. She needed to know at any given time one of us could pop up in Waterbury, Connecticut.

I didn't want to let her walk away, but apparently Carlos thought this was our best move. We cleaned her up and allowed her to leave even though my gut told me she would be a problem.

CARLOS

I had no need to kill Shaniqua, because she wasn't a threat. I even told her I was sorry for her loss. I know that probably didn't mean much since it was my sisters who killed her uncle, but it was the thought that counted.

There had been a lot going on in our family. I was dating my boy Ronnie's sister, Butta started fucking around with their cousin, Pep was creeping with the homie June and Ronnie thought I didn't know he was checking for Choc.

I was cool with June and Ronnie dating my sisters but they knew what lines not to cross. They were riders almost just like us, but we didn't put that out there like that.

Unfortunately my mom and Choc's mom was killed in a car accident, and we wanted the driver's head on a platter. We were already serious potheads and since our moms passed Chocolate is going harder than normal.

Butta found out a lot of information on the guy who killed our mother's. His name was Malik Meyers and he was the son of an ex-police chief that was apparently driving under the influence.

When Butta brought that information to me, I was livid and out for blood. I couldn't contain myself and I knew I had to do some damage; I mean his drunk ass killed our moms.

"So, this is all this nigga's fault?" I heard Pepper say.

"Looks like it," Butta replied.

"What y'all in here whispering about?" I asked.

They both jumped and it was obvious that they hadn't heard me open the door. Pep relied all dramatic and it was obvious her and Butta were hiding something. That's when they confessed all they knew about Malik Meyers.

When we decided to take care of Malik we ran into a snag. On top of our Grandmother's health diminishing, some old dude was home with Malik and called the police once we entered his home.

We were able to take out our target and his grandfather, but unfortunately the cops arrived. We all managed to get out the house, but once we made our way to the getaway car, it was obvious Choc wasn't with us.

We turned around to see if we could find her, but shots rang out and we took cover. Once we made our way back to the Meyer's house we seen my sister handcuffed to a gurney.

Pepper's tears flooded her face, and I rushed us all back to the house. We rushed home to figure out what was our next move and how could we help my sister. There was nothing we could do but get a lawyer and fight.

It had been more than a month and Chocolate was still locked up. There was no evidence left in the house but yet they still held her.

While she was locked up we had a whole different type of bullshit brewing and we had to end that shit real quick. I knew death was coming when I opened the door and Shaniqua was standing there.

"Bro…Butttttaaaaaa," I called out.

"I'm actually here to see you too," Shaniqua confessed.

"What's good?" I asked.

"My ex and my uncle were really close and he flew out here to do some digging," she stated.

"And?" Butta asked.

"He knows it was two females. When he called and told me that I hopped on the next available flight and came to California."

"Where is he?" I wondered.

"He is staying at the Marriot by the Long Beach Airport. His name is Kizzy," she stated.

I fell out laughing because what kind of nigga is named Kizzy. I knew a few bitches around the way with the same name but never a nigga.

I decided to go on a solo mission to check out this Kizzy character, but Pep had been so depressed with Chocolate being locked up I decided to bring her with me.

BUTTA

When my brother left to go check out the Kizzy character he left me and Shaniqua alone. You know a nigga like me rolled a blunt. Shaniqua was acting all sadity like she didn't want to hit the blunt. Once she calmed down she took a toke.

"That's some good weed huh," I asked.

"Uh huh," she meekly replied.

I had fucked her a few times so this meek shit was driving me crazy. I was grateful she informed us about Kizzy so I planned on giving her some good dick.

"You want to go to my room?" I asked.

A smile crept across her face, and I knew she was reminiscing on this dick. I didn't need to kiss or eat pussy today I was about to dig in those walls.

I stood her up and unbuttoned her pants. She got the hint and finished pulling them and her panties down. I grabbed a condom and stroked myself a moment to ensure I was fully erect.

Once the condom was on I bent her over and entered her already wet pussy. I was going to town, tearing Shaniqua's pussy up when Drea came to the door.

"Butta muthafucking Brown. Are you fucking a bitch?" she barked.

Drea had peep through the slit in the curtains and busted my ass. I knew it was about to be some shit because that girl was crazy. I understood LA crazy but Drea was from Chicago. I met her one year I went to visit Nico.

I dicked her down so good she moved to California. I wasn't mad at her move at all, she had some good pussy. Plus bitches seemed to move wherever I was.

I pulled out of Shaniqua and saw the horror on her face. When I got to the front door Drea was gone. I almost sighed with relief until I turned around and saw her entering the kitchen. I thought about the knives and my blade begins to twitch. I loved Drea but I'd gut her ass before she guts me.

"Who the fuck is this bitch?" Drea asked.

"Stop all that yelling and go wait in my room," I ordered.

I could tell Shaniqua wasn't a punk but she didn't know what Drea was capable of so she stood there and let me handle it.

"I ain't going nowhere till this bitch leave," Drea spat.

"I'm not going to be too many more bitches," Shaniqua spoke up.

My head spun around and I thought this bitch had balls. I'm sure Shaniqua could hold her own, but Drea ass should have been a Brown.

Drea was charging for Shaniqua and Shaniqua had got into her fight stance. I was at a loss for the first time. The man in me wanted to see them go at it, but I knew Carlos would pitch a fit about someone fighting at the house. Instead I grabbed Drea in a bear hug and damn near drug her to my room. She was clawing at my ass non-stop.

I apologized to Shaniqua and told her I'd be in touch. I couldn't get her out the house fast enough. There was no way in hell I could let Drea get her hands on that girl. I closed the door and it was on.

"I know the Brown men have reputations of being hoes, but really? In your house, knowing I have full access to your house."

I really didn't have an excuse and if you knew Drea once she's going in on someone there is no stopping her. I stood there listening to her rant. I knew she loved the dick so I thought if I fucked her she would shut up.

I walked closer to her and pulled her in for a kiss. I had a firm hold on that ass she was toting. Instead of returning the kiss she pushed me away.

"Don't put your nasty mouth on me after you been all up on that girl."

"I didn't kiss her."

I could have sworn her head turned around like the Exorcist. The steam that came from her head let it be known I was on pussy punishment for a while.

"What in the fuck is that supposed to mean? Your dick was just inside of her," she ranted.

We went back and forth for about an hour until Los came home. When she saw Los she stormed off. I wasn't even going to try and chase her; she really needed to calm down. We weren't exclusive but she made it be known that I was hers.

"What the hell wrong with Drea crazy ass," laughed Los.

"You don't even want to know," I replied while shaking my head.

He let me now that the bitch nigga Kizzy had been talking to the cops and trying to get to the bottom of Mr. Parking Lot's murder.

I knew I should call Shaniqua but in all honesty, I was scared Drea would know. I felt myself about to stress and grabbed me a blunt to spark up.

Los and I decided to just take care of Kizzy and leave Shaniqua out of it.

PEPPER

I was lost without Choc. Even though we didn't grow up together life was extremely hard without her. Things had gotten completely out of control.

We had the Kizzy drama, Choc was still locked up and the latest drama to add would be our so called crew was no more. June and Los had a bad altercation and you already know I was banned from talking to him. I wrote Choc to explain.

"Dear Choc,

Shit is real fucked up out here. Our family is falling apart and so are our friendships. Our crazy brothers beat the hell out of June and you know what that means. You know me; I would be all on their team if the shit wasn't petty. They fought over who would comfort me. Hahaha ain't that shit dumb. Now the mighty Brown boys have

given me an ultimatum, leave June alone or else. Girl I don't want to leave June alone he got that good dick. Hahaha. I know you're laughing your ass off right now, but it's true. I can't wait for you to come home, its lonely out here without you. I'm dealing with dumb and dumber all alone. Who knew having brothers was a full time job? I definitely didn't get the memo. Oh well, we will be visiting you soon.
Love and kisses, your sister Pep

We never had to make that trip to visit Choc, after all this time they dropped the charges and released her. I was ready to get fucked up. It was like Christmas, my sister was coming home.

As soon as she got home we were rolling blunts and pouring drinks. Choc tried to take a long bath but I wasn't having it. She even said she would wait to call her boo thang Ronnie in the morning. She just wanted to chill with her siblings for a little while. Unfortunately Ronnie decided to pop up the next morning.

I woke up to the smell of bacon, ham, eggs, waffles, biscuits and home fries. My brothers were showing off in the kitchen. Before heading to the kitchen I jumped in the shower. Threw on some simple blue jean Capri pants, with a white tank top and white flip flops.

"There she is," I sang.

"Yep here I am," Choc laughed.

"Hope you are hungry because we cooked the whole kitchen," Butta chimed in.

Carlos walked over to Choc and gave her a huge hug and a kiss on the forehead, "I missed you."

"Awww, I missed you too," she cried.

Even though she had three siblings, the bond between Carlos and Choc was unbreakable. Maybe it was because they were the first two to find each other or just because she's known of him longer. Whatever it was, it was strong.

"Get off my sister," I joked.

He was pulling Choc away from me as I pulled her closer to me. Butta ran to intervene, but instead of helping me he began yanking Choc towards him. Completely out of breath and oblivious to the fact that we were being watched, we pulled, yanked and laughed.

"Was anyone going to tell me Choc was home?" questioned Ronnie.

She turned around cheesing from ear to ear as I trotted to the door and unlocked it.

"Bayyyyybeeeee!" she yelled as she jumped into his arms. Carlos frowned and Butta laughed.

"When did you get home?" he quizzed.

"Late last night," she replied.

"You couldn't call me?" he continued to quiz.

He seemed more focused on the fact that Chocolate didn't call him last night than the fact that she was standing right here.

"I was going to call you this morning," she informed him.

"Hmmmph," he grunted.

"Hmmmph what?" I wondered. He never got a chance to answer me because our daddy oh I mean my brother started to dominate the conversation.

"Nigga stop questioning my sister!" he barked.

"Here we go," I warned.

"Nah it ain't here we go. Carlos need to gon' with that bullshit," Ronnie spat.

"I ain't gotta gon' with nothing. This is my house, last time I checked I didn't invite you over," Carlos stated.

"Hey I just got home, will you two play nice?" Chocolate asked.

Ronnie mumbled something as he walked outside and Carlos retreated to his room and grabbed a blunt and some weed.

"Damn Choc, Carlos actually listened to you. You must have the magic touch," I stated.

"Girl, he reminds me so much of daddy," Choc added.

My sister agreed and made her way to the porch to check on her man and his bruised ego.

"You alright?" she asked.

"I'm good but your brother is on one. It's been weeks and he still won't speak to June. He barely talks to

Saniyah. So she's all sad and shit," he informed Choc.

I felt bad for them, I knew dealing with my brother was a tough job, and no one did it as good as me. Not even Butta could calm his crazy ass down.

"I apologize for my brother; sometimes he is a bit overprotective. But he means well, "Choc said.

"Don't apologize for that nigga. He a grown ass man, he can speak for himself," Ronnie spat.

I looked at Ronnie like he was crazy. If he thinks my brother is overprotective he hasn't seen anything yet.

"Negro! Have you lost your mind? I say what the fuck I want to say. What you need to do is watch what the fuck you say about my damn brother! As a matter of fact you need to leave," Choc yelled.

This was Choc's first day home and drama was already unfolding. After Choc checked Ronnie's ass he tucked his tail and left. I didn't give a fuck we had food and weed to get back to.

CHOCOLATE

By the time I was home our lives were in turmoil, nothing felt the same, even Ronnie was crossing lines. We weren't super serious but he was the first guy I even considered calling my man since Larry and Charmaine's fucking fiasco.

When I was informed about this Kizzy character I was in complete shock, because I could have sworn this situation had been taken care of. Part of me wanted Shaniqua's head on a platter, but Butta swore she was innocent.

Then my brothers whoring around had crazy ass Drea doing pop ups all the damn time. Whatever pimp shit my dad was telling bitches my brothers sure did inherit it because these hoes will endure all kinds of bullshit to fuck with those two.

I'm not going to get into the whole my grandmother is a liar thing either. Okay well maybe a little bit. Did y'all know we've had been lied to our whole lives? Well you know that much because Papa was a rolling stone, but I mean my grandfather is alive. My dad's dad never died like they said and to top it off my dad had a *twin sister*.

Stop blinking like I'm crazy. You heard me loud and clear, he has a damn sister. Her name is Charlese; seemingly there was some family drama that drove a wedge between everyone.

Well Charles Brown Sr. has come out of hiding and brought his daughter too. He definitely was a leader but he was having trouble leading Carlos. My brother took his advice but made it clear that per my daddy's wishes he had full authority of his siblings.

I stood back to catch my breath and to figure out our next move. Technically Kizzy was mines and Pep's problem so I wanted to make sure we had a huge part in his termination.

Also June had flipped on everyone. I had to take Pep to have an abortion recently, the nigga was on that the baby ain't mines shit, but it was cool. His days were already numbered, especially since he put hands on Saniyah. If you don't remember, Saniyah is Ronnie's sister that Los is fucking.

We were plotting too many murders, but honestly we were excited. We discovered June and Charmaine had the same dad which was that bitch nigga Malik Meyers. That nigga June was on some revenge shit and I didn't even care, he could definitely get it. It was time he felt our wrath.

"Fuck the plans. Let's get that nigga tonight," I suggested.

"I'm with you on that sis," Butta replied.

Grandpa and Carlos were on board, so once again it's on. I wasn't comfortable with so many of us going, but we all wanted to be the one to dead this nigga. With that being said, I rolled us a blunt and we had the breakfast of champions...marijuana.

Later on that night we all headed to June's house. It was the weekend so we knew he got in from work around midnight. I don't know what it was but my brother's love taking people out in their own homes. When I heard June pull up we all got into position. He walked in and started shedding his clothes. He got to his room and hit the light.

"What the fuck? Pepper what are you doing here?" he quizzed.

"You don't miss me?" Pepper asked.

"I know what this is," June smiled. "Tell your brothers to come on out. If it's my time then it's my time," he stated with a smile.

"Fuck this shit," Butta said as he revealed himself.

June laughed a little, then one by one everyone else revealed themselves.

He looked around and seen everyone's faces.

"Now y'all are recruiting old folks. Fuck outta here," he smirked. The blood boiled in my veins, sweat poured from my forehead as I began to laugh. We knew June carried a piece but he made the mistake of stripping when he entered his home. He was in nothing but socks, boxers and a wife beater. My grandfather quickly grabbed him from behind. When June hit the floor, we were shocked to see him bleeding out. My grandfather had pulled the blade from his mouth and slit his throat all in one motion.

We were impressed with grandpa's skills and glad all this was coming to an end, or so we thought.

Once we got home we settled in and Charmaine's ass was still haunting me from the grave.

Her bitch of a mother showed up and wanted to cause havoc. She had the drop on my aunt but to our surprise my grandmother had snuck herself out of the convalescent home and saved the day.

When we first saw Char's mother Miss Monroe fall to her knee's we were confused then I saw Grandma in the shadows coming to save the day.

We ushered her in as Grandpa and Butta began the clean-up process. We were concerned about her health but she insured us she was fine.

"Y'all playing with fire living this here lifestyle," Grandma stated.

"We know what we are doing Granny," I assured her.

"At one point I thought the same thing."

She went on to break down our family history. It was strange to find out that my entire immediate family killed people for a hobby. After the strange feeling wore off I embraced how much of a bind we all truly had and was saddened our parents wasn't around to see this.

****

Now we were prepared to focus on that bitch nigga Kizzy. He had no clue what he had gotten himself into, but Shaniqua surely knew. She was excited that his days were numbered she said he was a nothing ass nigga she wish she never met.

"Don't worry about me keeping my mouth shut, you are actually going to be doing me a favor," she said with a smile.

I stared at her and she seemed genuine but my Grandpa had implemented the no witness rule and to me she was a liability. I didn't say anything since Los and Butta wasn't trippin'.

"As long as you keep your mouth closed I'm good," I replied.

After Shaniqua assured me we could trust her, we smoked a blunt with her and sent her on her way. We had to prepare to get rid of this fool Kizzy.

BUTTA

The time had come for us to off that nigga Kizzy but Drea was on her normal bullshit. She knew a nigga lived a gutter life, but was swearing up and down I was about to go over some bitch house. It took Pep and Choc to convince her that this was business. I had to make a new rule about bitches knowing where I lay my head.

We were suited and booted when Kizzy walked up to our porch and knocked on the front door. I looked out the screen and smiled. Glancing over to my siblings to get their attention, I let out a slight whistle.

When all our eyes recognized our target had delivered himself to us on a silver platter Chocolate sparked a blunt in celebration. We hated handling shit at home, but lately muthafucka's walked right into our home looking for trouble.

"May I help you?" Los asked.

"Are you the man of the house?" he asked.

"Yep, may I help you?"

"Can I come in and speak with you?"

"Are you the police? Or do you work for the police?"

"No, but I am investigating something on my own."

Los allowed him to enter and we closed the screen and the wooden door. I could tell he was uncomfortable when my sisters started to close the blinds and curtains.

"What the hell going on?" he wondered.

"You tell us," I replied.

"I just wanted to talk to the twins about something," he stated.

"There are no twins here," I replied.

"Those two," he pointed at Choc and Pep.

My sisters both let out a slight giggle, they were used to people assuming they were twins. They were the same age, height, weight, and complexion. If you didn't know them you would swear they were twins too.

"No we are not twins, but what do you want with us?" Pep replied.

"I have reason to believe you and your un-twin killed a very dear friend of mine," he stated.

"And what reasons are those?" Chocolate wondered.

"The fact that you came up in a few conversations," he smugly answered.

"Fuck the bullshit, what the fuck do you want," Pep snaps.

"You to confess," he smirked.

"I confess your ass is corny," laughed Choc.

"If you bitches had anything to do with..." he started saying.

I karate chopped that fool in the throat for disrespecting my sisters; plus he was on my bitch Shaniqua's shit list.

"That was for Shaniqua," I smirked.

He looked at me in disbelief; I guess he didn't know Shaniqua was that grimy. You piss a chick off enough you never know what she will have done to you.

He stood holding his throat and trying to catch his breath, he wasn't going to flex because he was outnumbered. He looked around at all of us and defeat sat on his face.

"Look, I don't want any trouble, all I do know is I'm barking up the wrong tree," he said while turning towards the door.

Pepper grabbed the steel bat that was by the door and Choc pulled a machete from the side of the couch, and then cut him off before he could make the door.

"Tell Shaniqua I'm sorry and I apologize for bothering you people," he stated.

"Quit being a bitch," I barked.

"Yes...yes...sir," he whimpered.

Carlos burst into laughter which made us all chuckle, my grandfather even had a little laughter slip out. Poor Kizzy stood their literally shaking. I wonder why people just can't seem to mind their own business.

"Buck up little boy," Grandpa ordered.

Kizzy was being such a bitch my grandfather wanted him to man the fuck up before he died. I already loved my grandpa he was amazing just like my father.

Before we continue with our little conversation my grandfather walked up to him and stabbed Kizzy in the eye. He opened his mouth to shriek and was caught with a bat to the ribs.

Kizzy fell to the floor and Choc hit him across the chest with the machete. Blood oozed out his chest as he began to shake viciously. Carlos gave him a swift kick to the head causing the shaking to slow down.

Aunt Charlese finished him off digging directly into his chest. We immediately moved to the clean-up process and body removal steps. Once everything was cleaned up, Carlos and I went to dump the body.

Our plan was to drive to an unfrequented area in the car he came over in and set it on fire. Carlos would follow me in his car then we would head back home.

Everything was going according to plan, the car was on fire and we were headed home. For some reason I asked Los to drop me off at Drea's house.

Something told me to go the hell home, but nah my ass had to go over there. I took the weed my brother had in the car, and headed in as he pulled off.

Drea gave me my own key a while back so I didn't have to knock. When I entered the house it was pitch black except for the light coming from her bedroom.

I casually walked to her room and instantly my blood began to boil. My blade slid from under my tongue and my heart was racing. Drea had a condescending smirk on her face.

"What the fuck going on in here?" I questioned.

"I just felt like having company," she smiled.

She was sitting there half dressed in some sort of nightgown and dude was fully dressed, but she knew better. The moment she gave me a key she knew she should not have invited a nigga over to her spot.

The nigga looked a little confused, he didn't know if he should leave or stay. His eyes went back and forth, between me and Drea.

"I'm in a real good mood my nigga. I suggest you leave while I'm offering it to you," I suggested.

He stood up but Drea pushed him back down. Each time he tried she was shoving him down on the couch. I was starting to get real pissed off.

"Nigga you stronger than a damn female, if you don't get the fuck up out of here you will be leaving in a body bag," I barked.

"He doesn't have to go anywhere, as long as you fucking other bitches, it's fair game."

He managed to get up and made his way towards the exit. Once he was gone she really went ape. We were arguing non-stop until she swung on me. I went out of my way to avoid hitting her but she kept provoking me.

I grabbed her by the neck and lifted her off the ground. I had no intentions on hurting her but she needed to be taught a lesson. She was kicking and squealing because she couldn't get a good scream out.

We were tussling all over her room. Even though I was manhandling her, I still prevented myself from knocking her ass out. This little bitch was strong too.

"Alright Drea calm the fuck down," I stated.

She ignored my ass and continued to tussle with me. I had her pinned down on her bed and she sent her knee flying into my side.

"FFUUUUUUCCCKKKKKK!!!!!!"
I yelled.

I released Drea and grabbed my side. When I removed my hand blood stained my palm. I looked at Drea and my blood pressure rose, right before my world slowly began to fade.

"Chocolate please get over here quick," I heard Drea say as darkness consumed me.

EXCERPT FROM BUTTA 2

CHOCOLATE

We had just arrived in Chicago and Butta's friend Nico was picking us up. He had all kinds of stories about my dad, and I enjoyed hearing them.

Pep and I whispered about how sexy Nico was. His girlfriend seemed cool but she was pretty silent.

It was my first time in Chicago and I wish it was under different circumstances. I don't know what made Drea think if she moved back to Chicago I wouldn't find her, but I'm about to prove her wrong.

Nico dropped us off at the hotel and told us he would be back in a few hours. I was cool with that but deep down inside revenge was calling.

Carlos was being extremely silent, I was grateful Nico left us some trees. I was in definite need of a blunt. I gave the marijuana to Pepper and she rolled us some smoke. The more we smoked the more I was ready to find Drea.

I called Nico back and told him we needed transportation or for him to come back sooner than later. Carlos knew we all needed more than some smoke in our system so he grabbed the ice bucket so he could go fill it.

He opened the door and standing across the hall putting her keycard in was none other than the infamous Drea. She slipped in her room hoping to be unnoticed and Los did the same.

"Little sisters our prayers have been answered, she's in the room across the hall.

BUTTA 2 COMING SOON

ALSO CHECK OUT

Creative Flow Publications

Author T. Hairston

Author Tywanda Brown

Author KeNetra

Author Simply Shonda

Author Valarie DeShazier